WORLD WAR I

THE GREAT WAR TO END ALL WARS

JULIE KNUTSON

ILLUSTRATED BY MICAH RAUCH

Nomad Press

A division of Nomad Communications

10 9 8 7 6 5 4 3 2 1

This book was manufactured by Versa Press,
East Peoria, Illinois, United States

June 2022, Job #J21-54435
ISBN Softcover: 978-1-61930-972-2
ISBN Hardcover: 978-1-61930-969-2

Educational Consultant, Marla Conn

Questions regarding the ordering of this book should be addressed to
Nomad Press
PO Box 1036, Norwich, VT 05055
www.nomadpress.net

Printed in the United States

Cover photo © IWM (Q 5935)

More World History Titles in the Inquire & Investigate Series

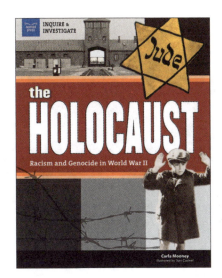

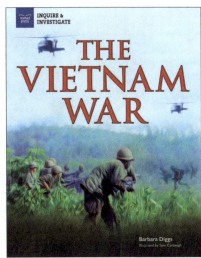

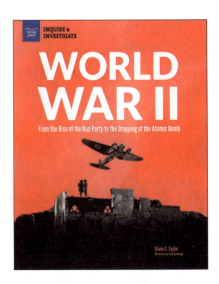

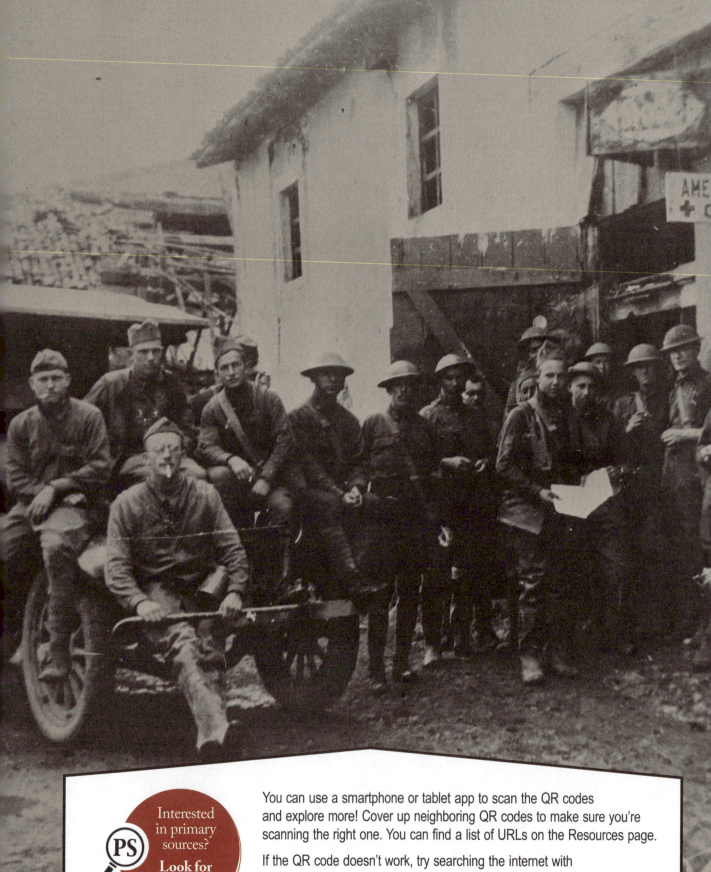

You can use a smartphone or tablet app to scan the QR codes and explore more! Cover up neighboring QR codes to make sure you're scanning the right one. You can find a list of URLs on the Resources page.

If the QR code doesn't work, try searching the internet with the Keyword Prompts to find other helpful sources.

Interested in primary sources? **Look for this icon.**

🔍 world war I

Contents

TIMELINE

1870–1871: A unified Germany emerges after the Franco-Prussian War.

1907: The second Hague Convention seeks to establish rules for modern warfare.

October 6, 1908: Austria-Hungary annexes the former Ottoman provinces of Bosnia and Herzegovina.

1912–1913: The Balkan Wars lead to major territorial losses for the Ottoman Empire. The stage is set for continued conflict over borders in the region.

Early 1914: Labor unrest grips much of Europe. In Russia, more than 1,450,000 workers strike in the first part of the year.

June 28, 1914: Austro-Hungarian Archduke Franz Ferdinand and his wife, Sophie, are assassinated by Serbian nationalists in Sarajevo.

July 23, 1914: Austria-Hungary issues an ultimatum to Serbia, giving it 48 hours to agree to the terms.

July 28, 1914: Austria-Hungary declares war on Serbia. Existing alliances lead Germany to join Austria-Hungary to form the Central Powers. Russia and France back Serbia in the conflict, forming the Allied Powers. Europe is engulfed in war.

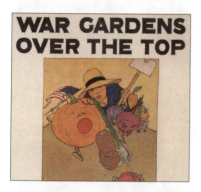

August 4, 1914: Germany invades neutral Belgium, drawing England into the war.

August 26–30, 1914: On the Eastern Front, Germany crushes Russia at Tannenberg, in East Prussia.

September 5–9, 1914: The Allies halt the advance of German troops on Paris, France, at the First Battle of the Marne.

October 28, 1914: The Ottoman Empire officially enters the war on the side of the Central Powers with attacks on Russian ports in the Black Sea.

December 25, 1914: At various points on both sides of the Western Front, soldiers lay down their arms in observance of a Christmas truce.

March 1915: The Ottoman government begins mass deportations of its Armenian minority population.

April 22, 1915: Poison gas is used as a weapon for the first time at the Second Battle of Ypres, in Belgium.

April 25, 1915: The Allied forces begin the ill-fated Gallipoli campaign in Turkey.

May 7, 1915: German U-boats torpedo the passenger liner RMS *Lusitania*.

May 31, 1916: Germany and Great Britain face off on the high seas in the Battle of Jutland, the major naval battle of the war.

September 15, 1916: Tanks debut on the battlefield at Somme, France.

January 22, 1917: U.S. President Woodrow Wilson argues for "Peace without victory."

February 1, 1917: Germany resumes unrestricted submarine warfare.

March 1, 1917: The Zimmermann telegram is released to the American public.

March 8, 1917: A series of protests and strikes rock Petrograd, Russia, sparking the Russian Revolution.

March 15, 1917: Tsar Nicholas II abdicates the throne in Russia. Power falls into the hands of a provisional government.

April 6, 1917: The United States declares war on Germany.

November 7, 1917: The Bolsheviks, a group led by Vladimir Lenin, seizes control in Russia.

March 3, 1918: Russia and Germany sign the Treaty of Brest-Litovsk, ending combat on the Eastern Front.

November 11, 1918: Germany signs the armistice agreement. The ceasefire goes into effect on the "eleventh hour of the eleventh day of the eleventh month."

1918–1919: More than 500 million people around the world are affected by an influenza pandemic.

January 4, 1919: The Paris Peace Conference begins, with representatives from 27 nations. Germany and Russia are not in attendance.

June 28, 1919: The Treaty of Versailles is signed by representatives from Germany and the Allies.

November 19, 1919: The U.S. Congress rejects the Treaty of Versailles.

MAP

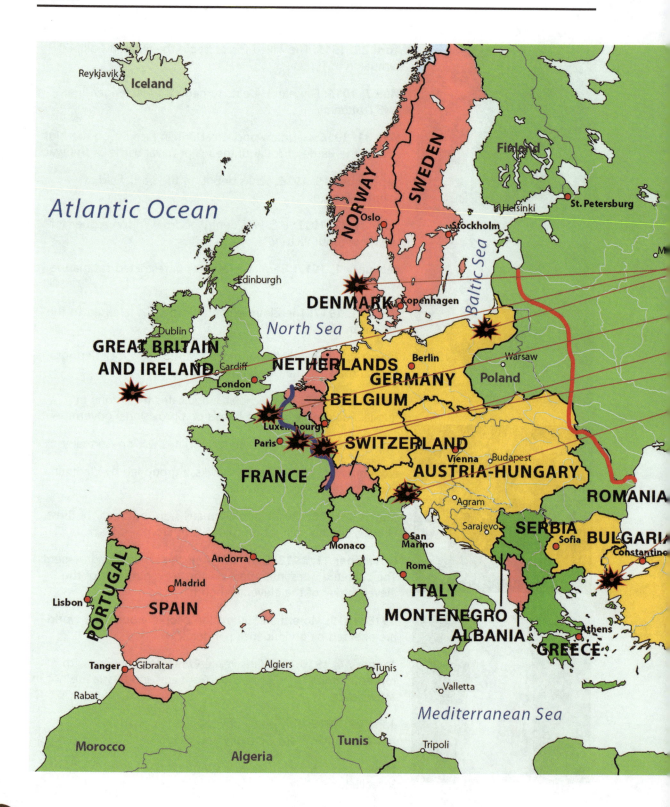

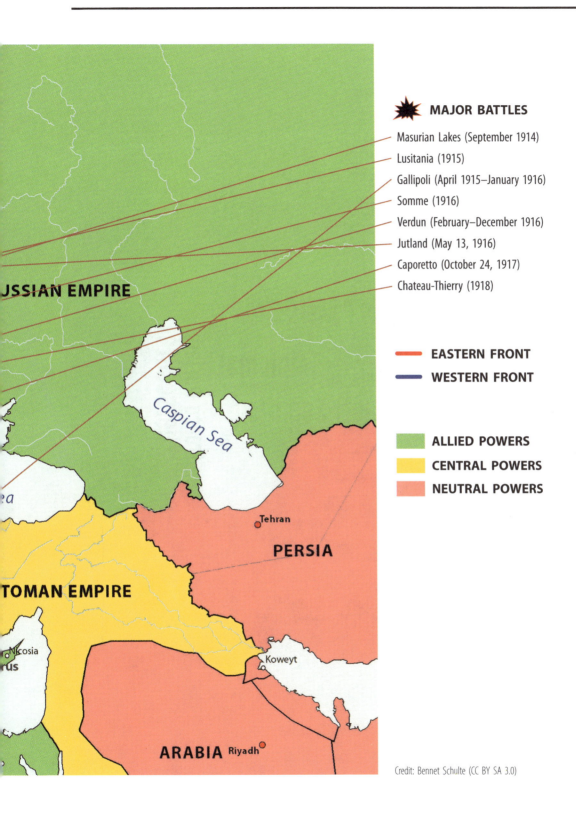

MAJOR BATTLES

Masurian Lakes (September 1914)

Lusitania (1915)

Gallipoli (April 1915–January 1916)

Somme (1916)

Verdun (February–December 1916)

Jutland (May 13, 1916)

Caporetto (October 24, 1917)

Chateau-Thierry (1918)

— **EASTERN FRONT**
— **WESTERN FRONT**

ALLIED POWERS
CENTRAL POWERS
NEUTRAL POWERS

RUSSIAN EMPIRE

Caspian Sea

Tehran

PERSIA

OTTOMAN EMPIRE

Nicosia

Koweyt

ARABIA   Riyadh

MAP   IX

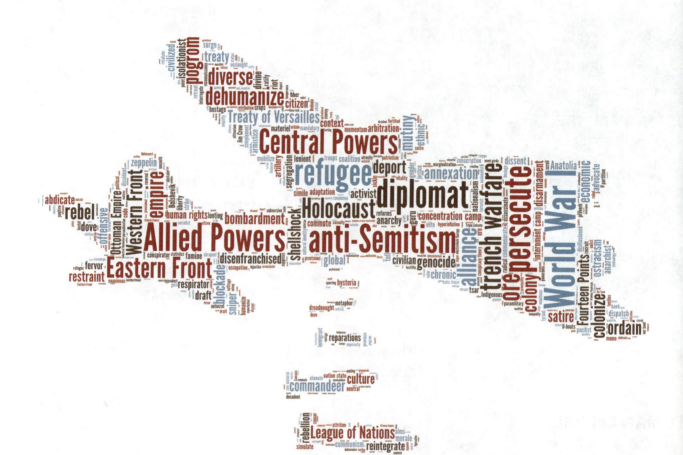

Introduction ▶

Beyond the War Room

How can citizens of the twenty-first century envision the realities of World War I?

More than 100 years after the war ended, it can be difficult to imagine the horrors of World War I. One way we can gain experiential knowledge of the events is through primary sources. These accounts from the actual time period help us better grasp what soldiers and civilians felt as the battles, surges, and retreats played out on the global stage.

A line of men snakes toward an invisible destination. Those in the foreground nearest to the viewer allow us a glimpse of their individual features and quirks. There's a sickle-carrying farmer sporting a red neck scarf and patterned cap. There's a judge clutching a scroll, white wig atop his head and black robe cloaking his body. Farther along, a golfer in a crimson jacket rests a club against his right shoulder. There are gentlemen wearing top hats and bowlers, carrying briefcases and picnic baskets.

With each step away from our vantage point, their individuality blurs. They become one, khaki-clad mass, steps and shadows in sync.

The poster begs all sorts of questions: Why are these men marching? What people and places are they leaving behind? What are they marching toward, what lies in that mysterious distance? Who isn't in line? What are the consequences of not stepping into place?

Four, simple words in bold blue letters call out from this British propaganda poster, designed to recruit soldiers for the "Great War" effort: "STEP INTO YOUR PLACE."

An English propaganda poster from World War I

THE DETAILS OF THE CONFLICT

World War I occurred between 1914 and 1918. What began as a nationalist conflict between Austria-Hungary and the tiny country of Serbia ballooned into a war involving 32 countries separated into two camps: the Allied and Central Powers. The core Allied Powers were Britain, France, and Russia, which backed the small, independent nation of Serbia. On the Central Powers side, Austria-Hungary brought its reliable friends—Germany and the Ottoman Empire—to the battlefields. Scores of other countries chose one side over the other, based on factors ranging from pre-war alliances to who seemed more likely to win.

THE PROPAGANDA MACHINE

Between 1914 and 1918, posters were used worldwide as propaganda tools. With striking visuals and graphics, they promoted patriotism and stoked fears of the enemy. The "Step into your Place" poster was used to recruit soldiers in England. Propaganda organizations reached potential soldiers in a variety of other ways and in a range of other locations, from soccer stadiums to movie theaters. Why do you think they advertised to people in places of fun and entertainment?

BATTLE LINES

When war broke out in 1914, Britain's soldiers needed to meet strict age and physical requirements. As the conflict wore on and death tolls rose, more troops were badly needed for combat. As a result, some requirements—such as those surrounding a soldier's height—were lowered.

Primary sources come from people who were eyewitnesses to events. They might write about the event, take videos, post messages to social media, or record the sound of an event. For example, the photographs in this book are primary sources, taken at the time of the event. Paintings of events are usually not primary sources, since they were often painted long after the event took place. They are secondary sources. Why do you think primary sources are important?

Troops in Russia during WWI

Battles were fought across Europe, Africa, the Middle East, Asia, and along the coast of South America. Fighting happened on land, in the skies, and on the open seas. The technologies used during battle, from submarines to machine guns to mustard gas, were new, untested, and capable of killing on a mass scale.

Estimates vary widely, but it is believed that a total of 9.7 million soldiers died and 12 to 13 million civilians perished. An additional 21.1 million were wounded and 7.7 million went missing, bringing military casualties to more than 40 million, a number unseen in human history.

BATTLE LINES

After two-and-a-half years of neutrality, the United States entered the war on the Allied side in April 1917. Though American troops began arriving in Europe in June 1917, they did not fully participate in frontline combat and trench warfare until October of that year.

Many civilian deaths were caused by the byproducts of war, including famine, disease, and genocide.

MORE THAN 100 YEARS LATER

It has been more than 100 years since the end of World War I. No longer a living memory, the generation of people who participated in this conflict, directly and indirectly, have largely passed on.

Today, we rely on a diverse collection of primary sources, including posters, films, letters, books, newspaper articles, government documents, and photos, to piece together the war's arc, magnitude, and impact.

From the United States to the Indian subcontinent, from Austria to Australia, war posters were everywhere during World War I. Before the rise of radio and television, posters offered a key way for governments to communicate with citizens. They were designed by teams of artists and marketing gurus to inspire patriotism and action and were plastered on buildings, in workplaces, and in subway cars. They also drew on stereotypes and symbols to amplify fear of the enemy. As curator David H. Mihaly told *Smithsonian Magazine* on the centennial of the war in 2014, "Posters sold the war." He explains, they "inspired you to enlist, to pick up the flag and support your country. They made you in some cases fear an enemy or created a fear you didn't know you had."

Take a look at some propaganda posters in this video. How do you hear about global events today?

PBS World War I posters

New Zealand troops in the trenches in France, 1917

Credit: Henry Armytage Sanders

BATTLE LINES

World War I is sometimes called the First World War, the Great War, or the War to End All Wars. The term "World War," or *Weltkrieg*, was first used in Germany in 1914.

Mining this trove of documents to re-imagine life between 1914 and 1918 is no small task, but we need to dust them off if we're to add color, depth, and context to our image of those bound for the front. We need to closely examine these documents if we are to humanize a conflict in which the loss of life was of such a mass scale that it can easily get reduced to a series of statistics.

Studying the history of World War I, or really any historical conflict, means engaging with different perspectives.

This is how we gain insight into how a few years can change the way people viewed their world and can also show us how events long past continue to shape our world.

Even today, the questions asked by contemporary human rights activists about the rules of engagement, such as the targeting of civilians during wartime and the use of chemical weapons such as poison gases, are rooted in this conflict. So, too, are questions about freedom of opinion in wartime and the role of governments in shaping public opinion through propaganda.

The map of the world as we see it was drawn as a result of this war. The twentieth century's most deadly genocide, the Holocaust of World War II, also traces its origins to this historical moment. From the landscape of the Middle East to the rise of communism in Russia, World War I's aftershocks were felt for decades. Many of the questions the war raised about injustice and persecution remain unresolved by today's world powers.

Examining the human dimension of World War I means looking at the accounts of real people who participated in the conflict in different ways. In this book, we turn to a range of primary documents to understand the war's causes. What motivations—political, economic, religious, intellectual—led leaders and civilians to the choices they made?

STEP INTO PLACE

The notion that young men should "Step into their place" wasn't limited to Great Britain. On all sides, recruits were told to set aside their individual hopes and ambitions for the national interest. A scene from the 1979 film adaptation of Erich Maria Remarque's 1928 novel, *All Quiet on the Western Front*, captures expectations in pre-war Germany. Early in the movie, a recent high school graduate who is reluctant to pack his things for the front stands before his teacher's desk. The teacher stresses that the time for play has passed. Now, he tells his former pupil, "the entire class will go as one man to serve the Fatherland." Why do you think that kind of expectation had so much power on young people? Do you think there is that kind of expectation of teenagers today?

VOCAB LAB

Write down what you think each word means. What root words can you find to help you? What does the context of the word tell you?

alliance, Allied Powers, Central Powers, genocide, nationalist, persecution, and **stereotype**

Compare your definitions with those of your friends or classmates. Did you all come up with the same meanings? Turn to the text and glossary if you need help.

TEXT TO WORLD

What do you know about the wars raging today? Do they affect your daily life? Why or why not?

Firsthand accounts bring into focus the nationalist fervor that convinced entire populations not only that they were superior to their neighbors, but also that those just beyond their borders were monstrous tyrants needing to be slayed. They point to the reasons why some world leaders believed war was politically and economically necessary. They also show why others thought war was a tool that governments were using to distract citizens from uniting around other problems, such as inequality and workers' rights.

Primary sources also help us understand the effects of the war. How did the war impact people and communities, and how did that impact vary by location, social class, race, age, and gender?

BATTLE LINES

The last known surviving veteran of World War I died on February 4, 2012, just shy of her 111th birthday. Florence Green served in Great Britain's newly formed Women's Royal Air Force (WRAF) during the war's last two months in 1918.

We begin by zooming out to observe the panorama of global relations in the years just before the war. Then, we telescope into the summer of 1914, examining the sequence of events that led to total war. Following that, we steady our focus on how the conflict played out on different fronts during the course of four years and look at the shaky resolutions that were reached in its aftermath. Finally, we reflect on the conflict's long-term impacts, examining how the world we live in today is one that this war made.

KEY QUESTIONS

* **What evidence supports the statement that World War I was a "global war"?**

* **What is propaganda, and what is one example of how governments used propaganda to shape public opinion during World War I?**

WORLD WAR I POSTERS

In a conflict of global scale, propaganda images that prove successful in one setting often migrate across oceans and continents. This happens today as well as in the past. In many instances, these visuals are adapted, remixed, and reused in new contexts for new audiences. Think of it as an early twentieth-century form of the meme!

- **Examine the gesture, posture, expression, and clothing worn by the central figure in each poster found at the links.**

  - What visual similarities do the images share? Why do you think this was a feature artists chose to reuse in different settings?

  - Are there familiar figures or symbols in the image? What power would the use of familiar visuals hold?

  - What visual differences exist between the images? What do the differences between the posters suggest about their audiences?

  - What words appear on the poster? Does the text relate directly or indirectly to the image?

- **Research the history of each poster.** Which was produced first? Where and by whom? For what purpose?

- **Make a timeline.** Show when, where, and by whom each poster was made, mapping its adaptation through the years.

Kirchner Britons

John Bull absent

Uncle Sam you

Canada war bonds poster

Daughters Zion recruit

To investigate more, visit a library or go online and research the history of the British War Propaganda Bureau (WPB) and the American Committee on Public Information (CPI). When did each group emerge? Who led them? What types of work did they create? Who were the audiences for these works of propaganda? How did they portray the enemy? Do we have anything similar today?

Inquire & Investigate

A DIFFERENT KIND OF BATTLEFIELD

In the early years of WWI, army recruiters mined soccer games and rugby matches for recruits. According to historian Adam Hochschild, soccer games "proved the single best venue for recruiters." Arriving spectators would see recruiters wearing sandwich boards bearing the message, "Your Country Needs You." The game would start with a patriotic speech. Players often stepped forward to enlist, and fans quickly followed their lead.

To investigate more, consider that the current military's recruiting efforts are increasingly digital. Platforms such as Instagram and e-sports sites are popular ways for reaching potential enlistees. Listen to or read the following piece from NPR. How are the tactics of today's military recruiters similar to those during World War I? How do they differ? Consider the language and imagery they use.

NPR army creative

- **Early in the war, the British newspaper _The Times_ published the following lines:**

  Come, leave the lure of the football field
  With its fame so lightly won,
  And take your place in a greater game
  Where worthier deeds are done . . .
  Come, join the ranks of our hero sons
  In the wider field of fame,
  Where the God of Right will watch the fight,
  And referee the game.

- **What is the "greater game"?** What lines justify the view that England has the support of a higher, divine power in wartime?

- **Take a look at posters advertising the Sportsmen's 1000 campaign, used in Australia.** Recruiters often presented war as another way of engaging in team sport "play." Who is targeted by this campaign? Whose image are they using for recruitment, and why? The image argues that sportsmen and soldiers share certain qualities. What are they?

Sportsmen's 1000 Australia

Chapter 1

Alliances Between Nations

What role did nationalism play in setting the stage for World War I?

As countries competed to become strongest in terms of industry, economics, and military might, their populations turned national pride into a way of feeling superior to other countries. When people from a neighboring nation are looked down on as lazy, dirty, or stupid, it's easier to support a war against them.

● ● ● ● ● ● ● ● ●

"It is a wide road that leads to war, and a narrow path that leads home." So goes an old Russian proverb. By 1914, the road to war in Europe was very, very wide. In fact, it could better be described as a multilane superhighway than a simple road. The continent's competing powers raced along this highway and, with each passing mile, countries eyed their neighbors with more and more hostility. Alliances formed out of suspicion, as leaders hoped to curb the economic growth, political power, and military strength of rival states.

In the globalizing world of the early nineteenth century, many factors fueled the race toward war. There were rising nationalist feelings, worsened ethnic tension, and ideas of cultural superiority and inferiority. Businessmen and politicians in industrializing countries scrambled to control colonies in Africa, Asia, and the Caribbean, hoping to use the resources and markets there as the foundations for their own fortunes and those of their home countries.

The rapid development of new military technologies presented other countries, including Germany, with the opportunity to flex their military muscles. In response, those countries lagging in the arms race, such as Russia, sought to halt that growing power.

On various home fronts, disenfranchised groups, including laborers and women's groups, took increasingly radical actions in their efforts toward equal rights and improved working and living conditions. This kind of organizing threatened to change the traditional balance of power in places ranging from France to England to Russia.

Some war hawks thought going to battle would help distract people from the domestic problems happening in their own countries. If these disenfranchised groups rallied around the call to war, the possibility of social, economic, and political revolution at home might be avoided.

This satirical, 1901 photo shows how gender roles were changing in the early twentieth century!

Credit: Underwood & Underwood

THE RISE OF A UNIFIED GERMANY

German unification resulted from the Franco-Prussian War (July 19, 1870–May 10, 1871). Before that, various kingdoms and principalities of German-speaking people existed independently, only loosely related. The Kingdom of Prussia, led by Otto von Bismarck (1815–1898), brought these independent states together to fight against France in 1870. After handily winning the war, the German kingdoms that fought together merged to form a single nation-state. The new country also included the territory of Alsace-Lorraine, annexed from France.

● ● ● ● ● ● ● ●

Today, historians still debate the causes of the Great War. Although the question "What caused World War I?" doesn't have easy answers, that doesn't mean we shouldn't ask it. Exploring the conditions that led to this conflict of unprecedented destruction matters as much today as it did more than 100 years ago.

POLITICAL FACTORS

At the outbreak of World War I, established empires entered the fight with the objective of preserving—and possibly expanding—their global status and wealth.

Emerging forces, whether the relatively new nation of Germany or nationalist groups seeking to build states based on ethnicity, sought to gain power.

During the 1700s and 1800s, new democratic republics in France, the United States, Haiti, and across Latin America had sprung up, raising questions of who had the right to rule. In these places, the idea of divinely ordained kings and queens who knew what was best for their subjects was replaced by the idea that all people had the right to life, liberty, property, and the pursuit of happiness.

In the century leading up to World War I, groups that had been historically silenced, including ethnic minorities, women, enslaved peoples, and workers' groups, all began to insist on their human rights. They demanded a voice and they demanded a vote.

BATTLE LINES

The term *war hawk* was coined during the War of 1812. U.S. Rep. John Randolph of Virginia used the label to refer to pro-war legislators. A contrasting term, *dove*, described those opposed to armed conflict.

Countries have no chance of winning wars if they don't have enough guns to fight. The gun industry in Great Britain boomed during the eighteenth century because there were so many wars.

Watch this video about the connection between industry and war. What's the connection between economic growth and war? What might this mean for today's world?

Stanford 18th-century British industrial

ECONOMIC FACTORS

As politics around the world were reshaped, new technologies radically changed the way that people lived and worked. With the Industrial Revolution, goods ranging from textiles to toys were produced on a mass scale. As the new powers of steam and machine grew and spread, economies transformed from agricultural to industrial and many people moved from rural areas to cities. Countries that were pioneers in industry, such as Great Britain, grew incredibly wealthy.

These new factories required a huge amount of raw materials, including metals, fuel, and fibers. New industrial powers took to the seas in search of places with plentiful resources where people and lands could be easily conquered. Other countries that were aiming to build competing industrial infrastructure took note of this success and joined the colonial race.

BATTLE LINES

The monarchs of Germany, Great Britain, and Russia shared common royal bloodlines. German Kaiser Wilhelm II (1859–1951), Britain's George V (1865–1936), and Alexandra Feodorovna (1894–1918), wife of Russian Tsar Nicholas II (1868–1918), were all first cousins who shared a common grandmother—Queen Victoria of England (1819–1901). They were all also fifth cousins, hailing from the line of England's King George II.

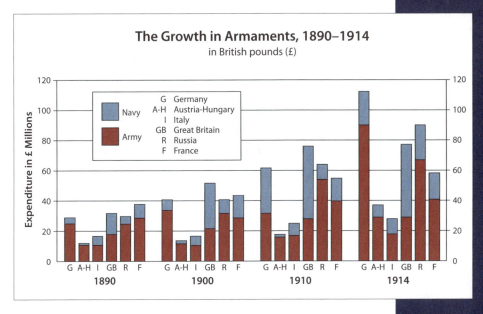

The Growth in Armaments, 1890–1914
in British pounds (£)

Expenditure in £ Millions

Navy
Army

G   Germany
A-H Austria-Hungary
I   Italy
GB Great Britain
R   Russia
F   France

G A-H I GB R F
1890

G A-H I GB R F
1900

G A-H I GB R F
1910

G A-H I GB R F
1914

This graph shows the increase in spending on munitions during the years leading up to World War I. Why do you think this was the case?

During this period of industrial transformation, the weapons of war changed as well. Low-tech bayonets and swords were replaced with efficient, factory-made magazine rifles and machine guns. These new tools of combat could kill many more people in a shorter span of time than the traditional, single-fire weapons.

Great Britain tested these new munitions in colonial conflicts in Africa, such as the Boer Wars during the late nineteenth century. Russia and Japan also experimented with machine guns and other instruments of modern war during the Russo-Japanese War of 1904–1905.

It was the dawn of a new age for warfare, and many of the old rules of engagement no longer applied. Europe's powers raced to be the best armed—to both defend themselves and to expand their empires.

CULTURAL FACTORS

As economic competition grew more intense, nations sought to define themselves and the people within their borders as distinct. Culture became a way for countries to express their differences and ideas of superiority.

The result of this celebration of culture was the circulation of dehumanizing stereotypes in images and words.

Here are some popular misconceptions of the time: Russians are uncouth and backward, the French are decadent and un-Christian, Germans are monstrous bullies. Why did people believe these lies?

Part of the reason was that this allowed people on one side of a border to view themselves as more humane and more civilized than their neighbors on the other side. For example, on both sides of the English Channel, popular culture made the threat of invasion seem extremely close.

In England, books such as *The Riddle of the Sands* (1903) brought a German invasion of the island to life in words. In Germany, the same rumors of invasion swirled. Worried parents in coastal towns sometimes even kept children home from school when raiding British forces were rumored to be just offshore.

BATTLE LINES

During the early 1900s, some argued that Europe's industrial powers were too economically interconnected for war to make sense. Why do you think this might have been a factor in preventing war? Do you think it would make a difference today?

French satirical cartoon map of Europe in 1870. How are the characters supposed to be reflective of their countries?

Credit: Paul Hadol

THE EVE OF WAR

With suspicions swirling and peace seeming more and more fragile, countries formed protective alliances. During the early 1880s, Germany feared those who wanted to see its new nation fail would sabotage the new state. This fear led it to form a pact with Austria-Hungary and Italy.

Germany's perceived aggression and growing military strength led France and Russia, which shared borders with Germany, to enter into an alliance in 1892. Great Britain and France, too, formed an agreement. In 1907, France, Russia, and Great Britain merged into an alliance known as the Triple Entente. As a result of these alliances, if conflict broke out between two of the powers, all signatories would be obligated to take part in the conflict.

These were just some of the conditions that set the stage for a war of unprecedented scale.

Russian poster showing female personifications of France, Russia, and Britain, 1914

TEXT TO WORLD

What is your cultural identity? How do you celebrate it without being offensive to other identities?

KEY QUESTIONS

- **Why did the Industrial Revolution spark a competition among European nations for colonial expansion?**

- **How did the alliances formed between European countries in the late 1800s affect the size and devastation of the war? What might the war have been like if countries hadn't made these agreements?**

COLONIAL CARTOGRAPHY

In the space of 20 years in the late 1800s, 90 percent of Africa fell under European colonial rule. This was a landmass four times larger than Europe. How did it happen?

- **Look at the map from 1880.** Note that "Br." stands for Great Britain, "Fr." stands for France, "Ot." stands for the Ottoman Empire, "Por." for Portugal, and "Sp." for Spain.

scramble for
Africa map

- **Compare the map from 1880 to that from 1913.** What changes do you note between the borders and boundaries of the map from 1880 and 1913? Consider the following:

  - European countries with African colonies in 1880.

  - Independent African states in 1880.

  - European countries with African colonies in 1913.

  - Independent African states in 1913.

- **How does the map change during these years?** What European countries seem to have the largest colonial holdings in Africa in 1880?

- **The remapping of the African continent resulted largely from the Berlin Conference of 1884.** Use the internet and books from your local library to research this conference.

  - Why was the Berlin Conference held?

  - What countries were involved?

  - What decisions were reached at the conference? How and why were these decisions reached?

  - Why did African people have no say in the future of their lands? Does this happen today?

To investigate more, consider that different European powers took different approaches to colonial governance. The regime of Belgium's King Leopold II in the Congo was marked by mass atrocities that were committed in pursuit of ivory and rubber. Research the history of Leopold's Free Congo State. Investigate when, how, and by whom its human rights violations were exposed.

To investigate more, consider that Serbia, Bulgaria, Romania, and Albania are not on the 1870 map, but are on the 1914 map. Research when, why, and how these new countries formed in the area known as the Balkans. What role did nationalism play in their formation?

SATIRE IN THE PRE-WAR YEARS

Satire is a form of social criticism. It can take the form of plays, literature, song lyrics, or cartoons, using humor to draw attention to social issues such as greed and government corruption. Let's take a look at a political cartoon from 1914.

The political cartoon "Map of Europe" was created by German-Jewish artist Walter Trier in 1914. Two renderings of Europe exist side-by-side: one from 1870, the other from 1914. You can examine the cartoon at this website.

Walter Trier BL

- **On the 1870 side, labels and place names are written in French.** On the 1914 side, they are written in German. Why might Trier have made that switch?

- **What new places appear on the 1914 map that are not on the 1870 map?**

- **Describe Germany and Austria Hungary's personification in the 1914 map.** What are the two powers doing? To whom?

- **Using the internet and library, investigate the causes and outcomes of the Franco-Prussian War of 1870-71.**

  - Why did this war begin? How long did it last?

  - Where was it fought?

  - Who won, and what were the consequences of victory?

- **Now, look at the cartoon again.** Revisit the question about Trier's use of French and German. Why would he have switched the language used to label the 1870 and 1914 versions of the map?

Chapter 2 ▶
The Dominoes Fall

WHEN WWI BROKE OUT, MY GREAT-GRANDPA SAID HE FELT IT WAS HIS DUTY TO HELP DEFEND HIS COUNTRY. HE ALSO THOUGHT IT WOULD JUST BE AN ADVENTURE THAT WOULD BE DONE BEFORE CHRISTMAS. UNFORTUNATELY, THAT TURNED OUT NOT TO BE TRUE AT ALL.

What effect did Archduke Franz Ferdinand's death have on the rest of the world?

While it might seem as though the murder of Archduke Franz Ferdinand of Austria and his wife sparked the war, in reality, the governments of several countries were already close to the boiling point. The deaths of these two people simply supplied the excuse they needed to declare war.

● ● ● ● ● ● ● ● ●

On June 28, 1914, two shots fired at close range in the Balkan city of Sarajevo killed Franz Ferdinand (1863–1914), heir to the sprawling Austro-Hungarian Empire, and his wife, Sophie (1868–1914). Throughout the five weeks that followed, kings, diplomats, military leaders, and citizens across the world reacted to the tragedy.

Would Austria-Hungary retaliate against the small and newly independent country of Serbia? Was all-out war inevitable or could the conflict be resolved in more peaceful ways? Could eruption be contained within the Balkans or would Europe's other "Great Powers," including Germany, Russia, France, England, and Italy, add to the tensions?

From the rear-view mirror through which we view all of history, we know that the dispute quickly spiraled. From a conflict between Austria-Hungary and Serbia it became one involving other major, European powers.

SHOTS IN SARAJEVO

Just a few days before visiting the Bosnian capital of Sarajevo to observe military trainings in June 1914, Franz Ferdinand remarked, "I wouldn't be surprised if there are a few Serbian bullets waiting for me." The 50-year-old Austrian archduke knew that he was stepping into an explosive minefield. Franz Ferdinand was set to soon inherit the throne from his aging uncle, Franz Joseph I (1830–1916).

BATTLE LINES

British Foreign Secretary Sir Edward Grey (1862–1933) predicted, "From the moment the dispute ceases to be one between Austria-Hungary and Serbia and becomes one in which another great power is involved, it cannot but end in the greatest catastrophe that has ever befallen the continent of Europe."

The archduke's goodwill trip to Bosnia's capital was well-publicized.

During their visit, Franz Ferdinand and Sophie were scheduled to participate in a parade and reception at Sarajevo's city hall. Announcements of their plans appeared in newspapers months in advance, and friends and foes alike took note . . . including a small group of young men in the Serbian capital of Belgrade.

All college students, these men wanted an ethnically unified Serbia free from foreign control. They had momentum following Serbia's victories in the Balkan Wars, after which the start-up state doubled its territory and increased its population from 3 million to 4.5 million. These young men were also influenced by the terrorist organization The Black Hand, which called for any means necessary to free the Balkans of foreign rule.

A MULTICULTURAL EMPIRE

The Austro-Hungarian Empire sprawled over much of Central and Eastern Europe. At least 10 different ethnicities lived within its borders. These groups included not just Austrians and Hungarians, but also Czechs, Slovaks, Poles, Romanians, Italians, Croatians, and Bosnians. With unique cultures, histories, and language traditions, many of these groups sought nationhood and self-rule.

SOPHIE AND FRANZ

They were the William and Kate or Harry and Meghan of the turn of the twentieth century. During the summer of 1900, American newspaper readers swooned over the marriage of Franz Ferdinand, heir to one of Europe's oldest houses, to Sophie Chotek, a woman of noble but lesser rank. The triumph of love was praised with headlines such as, "Austrian Archduke Franz Ferdinand Prefers True Love to His Children's Heritage."

● ● ● ● ● ● ● ● ●

What exactly were the rebels upset about? Land.

The Balkan Peninsula is a jigsaw-shaped landmass in Europe's southeastern corner. In the nineteenth century, new nation states—Bulgaria, Greece, Montenegro, and Serbia—gained independence from the Turkish Ottoman Empire. Still, some parts of the Peninsula remained under Ottoman control.

These new countries banded together to defeat the Ottoman Empire, fighting the First Balkan War in 1912 and 1913. The Balkan countries won, and the Ottomans lost 83 percent of their territories in Europe. Bulgaria, the main victor, was unhappy with how land seized from the Ottomans was divided. The Second Balkan War, during the summer of 1913, positioned Bulgaria against Serbia and Greece.

The following summer, when Franz Ferdinand visited the Austro-Hungarian territory of Bosnia, tensions were high. Austria-Hungary had occupied this region from 1878 onward and officially annexed it in 1908–1909. Given that the province had a large population of ethnic Serbs, Serbian nationalists wanted to bring it under their control. The stage was set for a spark to grow into a gigantic fire.

The morning of June 28 was one of anniversaries. Franz and Sophie Ferdinand were celebrating the 14th anniversary of their announcement of marriage. Ethnic Serbs in the city were commemorating the Battle of Kosovo that happened in 1389, a failed Serbian uprising against the Ottoman Turks.

For many Serbs, this anniversary provided a chance to remember Serbia's long struggle to free itself of foreign oppression. Because of this, many observers saw the archduke's visit as poorly timed.

A drawing by Achille Beltrame depicting Gavrilo Princip killing Archduke Franz Ferdinand of Austria in Sarajevo, 1914, from the *Domenica del Corriere*.

After arriving at Sarajevo's train station, the royal couple set out in a convoy of vehicles. All along their announced route, six assassins waited. The first man watched the pair's convertible car roll past, but failed to pull the trigger of his gun. The next, a young man dying of tuberculosis, launched a bomb that bounced off the archduke's automobile. The bomb exploded under the car behind Franz Ferdinand's, injuring 20 people. The would-be assassin was arrested before he could take his own life.

THE HOME RULE CRISIS

Viking raids, Norman conquests, English colonization . . . the bid for Irish self-rule was centuries in the making. It reached a crescendo between 1912 and 1914, when Irish nationalists, who wanted sovereignty, and unionists, who wanted to maintain links to England, clashed in what's known as the Home Rule Crisis. Paramilitary groups on both sides imported guns from Germany as simmering tension flared into militant action. The outbreak of war in August 1914 halted discussion of the "how" and the "when" of Irish independence. Those questions would have to wait until the end of World War I. After the war, their lack of resolution led to the Irish War of Independence (1919–1921), the Irish Civil War (1922–1923), and a century of continued conflict between Catholics and Protestants on the island.

Shaken, Franz and Sophie Ferdinand were rushed to the safety of the town hall. There, the archduke delivered a speech from paper speckled with the blood of those wounded in the attack. He then requested to visit the injured at the hospital.

After leaving the town hall, their driver made a wrong turn along the route. Franz Ferdinand's car stopped at a corner, right in front of one of the four remaining terrorists who had planned to kill the monarch. This young man, Gavrilo Princip (1894–1918), raised his gun, first shooting Sophie and then the archduke. They were both mortally wounded.

These were the first two fatal shots of the First World War.

THE WORLD REACTS

On Monday, June 29, 1914, newspapers around the world shouted notice of the assassination. Many journalists and cartoonists presented it as the most recent in a long line of tragic incidents to happen to Austria-Hungary's ruling family. In Berlin, the *Berliner Lokal-Anzeiger* reported that the news hit "like a lightning strike." In Vienna, many viewed the murders as an invitation to armed conflict with Serbia.

For some of the men advising the reigning monarch Franz Joseph, the situation demanded immediate action. Oskar Potiorek (1853–1933), a high-ranking military officer who was riding in the car at the time of the assassination, told his superiors, "Serbia must learn to fear us again . . . or our old border regions, and not just the annexed provinces, will be in danger."

And while certain officials in Germany, Austria-Hungary's ally, urged calm restraint, Kaiser Wilhelm (1859–1941), a close friend of Franz Ferdinand's, believed that "the Serbs must be sorted, and that right soon!"

Even though many European leaders were on holiday in early July, conversations between Austria-Hungary and Germany took place in secret throughout the first part of the month. They happened in person, by letter, and by telegram.

Mexico was the scene of armed revolutions between 1910 and 1920 that transformed both government and culture. Among the leaders of the insurgency were Emiliano Zapata and Pancho Villa (third from right).

Within weeks, a plan was set to serve Serbia with an ultimatum. Serbia would need to agree to certain conditions and demands in order to prevent war. Knowing that Russia would likely rally to aid its Slavic ally, the release of the ultimatum was delayed. This would limit the time that Russia and its partner, France, had to mobilize their militaries.

On a practical level, the timing also allowed Austria-Hungary to harvest the crops that would feed its soldiers.

From early to mid-July, the conflict largely slipped from the front pages of American and Canadian newspapers. In North American newspapers—from St. Louis to Scranton to Saskatchewan—it was replaced with news of revolution in Mexico and reports of conflicts between England and Ireland.

You can read an English translation of the ultimatum at this website.

Why do you think Austria-Hungary and Germany made the ultimatum very demanding?

lib Austro Hungarian ultimatum

French soldiers guard a subway entrance in Paris, France, at the beginning of World War I.

From 1914 to 1818, Belgrade's male physicians were conscripted in service of Serbia. Slavka Mihajlović (dates unknown), a 26-year-old female doctor, was the only physician to continue working in all departments of the General State Hospital. Mihajlović's war diary was published in 1955 as *Clouds Over the City.*

You can learn more about her and read selections from the diary here.

Slavka Mihajlović

In England, Russia, and Germany, the first part of 1914 had been marked by political unrest on the home front. In all three settings, labor groups pushed for their rights and for unity among the workers of the world. In England, Irish independence was a major question, as were women's rights.

When Austria-Hungary finally issued its ultimatum on July 23, socialists in Germany and England were still protesting the prospect of war. Activists such as Rosa Luxemburg (1871–1919) in Germany even advocated for a general workers strike if the country's legislature approved war funds. She noted that the majority of those fighting the war would be from the laboring class, known as the proletariats.

In her view, their efforts would be better spent uniting as workers rather than spilling each other's blood on battlefields.

THE ULTIMATUM IS ISSUED

When the ultimatum arrived in Serbia's capital, Belgrade, it contained terms that nearly all observers knew would be unacceptable. The document demanded that the Serbian government admit it tolerated terrorist activity. It also demanded that Serbia accept Austria-Hungary's annexation of Bosnia and issue an apology in the pages of the country's newspapers. It further required Serbia to restrict criticism of Austria-Hungary, both in the press and in schools.

Why do you think this was one of the demands?

Serbia was given 48 hours to respond. The Serbian government agreed to nearly all of the demands and asked to come to the conference table with Austria-Hungary for negotiations. With backing promised from Germany, Austria-Hungary rejected the request.

On July 28, one month to the day after the assassination, Austria-Hungary declared war on Serbia. Bombs began to fall in Belgrade. As Serbian doctor Slavka Mihajlović recorded in her diary, "The explosion echoes around Belgrade and the hospital shakes. We all jump out of bed, more out of astonishment than fear, and stay up till dawn. So it is true! The war has started! Big Austria has moved against small war-torn Serbia!"

BATTLE LINES

In the areas surrounding Berlin, more than 2,000 couples rushed to get married the weekend war was announced.

FRANCE BEFORE RUSSIA

The Schlieffen Plan was the brainchild of military strategist Count Alfred von Schlieffen (1833–1913). His plan of attack targeted France first because that country's network of roads and rails would allow it to quickly train and mobilize soldiers to battlefields. France was also an immediate threat because its border was so close to many German industrial cities. Capture of those manufacturing centers by the enemy would spell catastrophe for the German economy and would limit the production of goods needed for war. In contrast, Russia had a relatively underdeveloped infrastructure, with poor rail and road systems. This meant that it would take longer to prepare troops and transport them to the front. To Schlieffen, the best course of action was to target France first and then shift focus to the east.

As historian Annika Mombauer explains, "Not everyone wanted to prevent a war, not everyone considered it the worst-possible outcome of the July Crisis, and some were willing to risk war rather than risk a decline in their international status."

From that moment, the dominoes quickly fell. Expecting the conflict to balloon, Russia began mobilizing troops in late July. Germany demanded that Russia stop mobilization. The demand was ignored, and Germany declared war on Russia on August 1.

Russia's ally, France, then readied its troops. This action led France and Germany to declare war on each other on August 3. When Germany released plans to invade neutral Belgium on August 4 in order to reach France, England entered the fray. The Central Powers—Austria-Hungary and Germany at their core—were now engaged in full-fledged war with the Allied Powers of Russia, France, and England within just a week after the ultimatum.

All of the nations involved expected it to be a quick war.

For years, their military strategists had developed plans of attack for a European war. For example, Germany's Schlieffen Plan called for fighting on two fronts. First, Germany would attack France on the Western Front. If all went according to plan, German troops would invade France through Belgium and Paris would be in German hands in six weeks. Then, Germany would turn its attention east to knock out Russia.

France's Plan XVII was a strategy for defeating Germany that French military leaders began to develop in 1911. It called for offensive attacks on German industrial areas near the French border. Plan XVII's engineers predicted an end to the conflict by Christmas 1914.

BATTLE LINES

Socialists believed in an international unity of workers that was more powerful that national allegiances. At the outset of war, many thought that this philosophy would lead socialists to resist fighting for their country. In France, this proved false. Based on political views, the government expected 13 percent of reservists not to report for duty. In reality, only 1.5 percent failed to do so. Why do you think this was the case?

EUROPE MOBILIZES

With Kaiser Wilhelm promising that troops would be home "before the leaves fall," young men across Germany rushed to enlist. In England and France, the rallying cries of war were equally effective. Across Europe, a romantic view of war as a not-to-be-missed adventure was widespread. Massive patriotic rallies and demonstrations seized the nations' capitals.

In Paris, President Raymond Poincaré (1860–1934) delivered an address to Parliament, noting, "Our nation is in arms and trembling with eagerness to defend the land of our fathers." Many organizations and publications that had opposed the war just days earlier switched sides and vowed loyalty to the government.

COUNTRIES IN FIRST WORLD WAR	STANDING ARMIES & RESERVES IN AUGUST 1914	MOBILIZED FORCES IN 1914–18
Russia	5,971,000	12,000,000
France	4,017,000	8,410,000
Great Britain	975,000	8,905,000
Italy	1,251,000	5,615,000
United States	200,000	4,355,000
Japan	800,000	800,000
Romania	290,000	750,000
Serbia	200,000	707,000
Belgium	117,000	267,000
Greece	230,000	230,000
Portugal	40,000	100,000
Montenegro	50,000	50,000
Germany	4,500,000	11,000,000
Austria-Hungary	3,000,000	7,800,000
Turkey	210,000	2,850,000
Bulgaria	280,000	1,200,000

At the beginning of World War I, the world's standing armies varied widely in size and readiness.

MORE PEOPLE NEEDED

In August 1914, Great Britain had only a small volunteer army. Secretary of War Horatio Herbert Kitchener (1850–1916) appealed to the public for 100,000 new recruits. Men lined up by the hundreds across England to join the ranks. Voluntary enlistment continued through 1915, with 2,446,719 men responding. Those numbers weren't enough. In January 1916, mandatory conscription was introduced. All single men between ages 18 and 41—except for teachers, clergymen, certain essential industrial workers, and the medically unfit—needed to register for service. While unpopular, this order resulted in an additional 2.5 million enlistees during the course of the war.

Many big questions on Europe's various home fronts—about Irish self-rule in England, women's right to vote, and workers' rights—were put on hold in the rush to defend the nation.

The fear that the "war would be over before it began" was soon disproved. As the first weeks showed, the plans laid by military leaders did not lead to a quick or bloodless victory. Writer Sir Arthur Conan Doyle (1859–1930) memorialized the first month of the war as the "most terrible August in the history of the world." It was just a small window into the destruction to come.

Just a month passed between the assassinations in Sarajevo and the formal declaration of war. Although there were diplomatic exchanges—including a series of letters between cousins Kaiser Wilhelm and Nicholas II—it was hard to halt a conflict decades in the making.

By early August, England rallied its population around the ideas of honor, duty, preservation of the past, and assurance of future stability.

In Germany, the war drum beat to the promise of spiritual renewal and national vitality through victory. These two different motivations toward war drove the conflict into its next chapter.

BATTLE LINES

In England, a group of pro-war women organized under the banner of the Order of the White Feather. Members of the group would pin white feathers on men they encountered on the street. The aim? To publicly shame them for not being engaged in overseas combat.

TEXT TO WORLD

Do you know anyone who serves in the military? What are their thoughts about armed conflict?

KEY QUESTIONS

- **Why did Gavrilo Princip and his co-conspirators target Archduke Ferdinand?**

- **What led so many European countries to enter into the conflict between Austria-Hungary and Serbia?**

- **Why did people across Europe expect the war to end quickly?**

GAMES AND PROPAGANDA

During the second half of the nineteenth century, the sweeping social and economic changes of urbanization and industrialization led Europe's growing middle classes to enjoy more leisure time. This trend allowed many to pursue new hobbies and activities. Sports such as soccer, rugby, bicycling, and cricket gained in popularity. Professional teams formed, cheered on by ferociously loyal fans. Europeans also enjoyed the thrills of newly built amusement parks in resort towns, read novels, newspapers, and magazines, and played games at home. Games were produced on a mass scale and were often designed to teach lessons and promote certain virtues.

- **Read the following essay that documents children's games in Austria-Hungary.** As you read, ask yourself the following questions.

Habsburger child's play

  - Why were these games developed?

  - What was their intended effect?

  - How did they represent the enemy? What impact might that representation have had on children as they grew into adults?

- **Today, games such as Risk, Battleship, and Axis & Allies offer players a simulated experience of developing wartime strategy.** Research these games.

  - When, where, and why did they emerge?

  - Do they teach specific lessons?

  - How are they similar to and different from the games that some Austro-Hungarian children played during World War I?

To investigate more, read how children's experiences of war were shaped by propaganda in the form of games, books, and toys and through organizations such as the Scouts. How did all of these types of leisure help support the war effort in England?

BL WWI children propaganda

Inquire & Investigate

▶

ANTI-WAR VOICES

Although many people and groups who held anti-war views in July 1914 eventually supported the government and its decision to go to war, some continued to hold pacifist positions after the outbreak of war. They did so even at risk to themselves and their families.

- **Research the following well-known anti-war figures to learn more about their lives.** What different reasons did they have for opposing the war? What sacrifices did they make for the sake of their beliefs?

  - Rosa Luxemburg (Germany)

  - Jean Jaurès (France)

  - Emma Goldman (U.S.)

  - Eugene Debs (U.S.)

  - James Keir Hardie (England)

  - Emily Hobhouse (England)

  - Bertrand Russell (England)

  - John Chilembwe (British colonial Africa/Nyasaland; modern-day Malawi)

- **Make a short documentary or podcast on one of these figures to introduce their life to new audiences.**

> To investigate more, consider that despite threats of imprisonment, physical violence, and social marginalization, prominent pacifists argued against war from its first days in the summer of 1914 through its November 1918 end. Did this phenomenon occur in more recent wars? Do some research into World War II, the Vietnam War, and the War on Terror to answer this question.

VOCAB LAB 📖

Write down what you think each word means. What root words can you find to help you? What does the context of the word tell you?

annexation, **conscription**, **convoy**, **proletariat** , **socialist**, and **ultimatum**

Compare your definitions with those of your friends or classmates. Did you all come up with the same meanings? Turn to the text and glossary if you need help.

Chapter 3 ▶

All's Not Quiet on the Western Front

IS THIS A PICTURE OF YOUR GREAT-GRANDPA AND HIS FRIEND?

Why did trench warfare take hold in late fall of 1914?

As war began, citizens thought it would be a short one, but by fall it was clear that no one would be going home before Christmas.

Instead, the different sides of the conflict dug trenches and hunkered down to a pattern of waiting and fighting.

● ● ● ● ● ● ● ● ●

In early August 1914, 550 westbound trains loaded with troops and equipment, their sides scrawled with messages such as "Day trip to Paris," rolled across Germany each day toward Belgium. Students and shopkeepers, farmers and philosophers, nearly 1.5 million soldiers bid farewell to families and friends in villages, towns, and cities.

In these early weeks of war, similar scenes played out across France and England. Young men said goodbye to family and headed to the Western Front. Within months, they were joined by colonial forces from places as far away as India, Algeria, Canada, Australia, Senegal, and Morocco.

In Belgium and France, citizens of border towns prepared for the coming war. In a panicked rush, they hurried to buy food and provisions. Their leaders destroyed infrastructure such as bridges, tunnels, and railroads, hoping to stall the advancing German forces. How would the conflict transform their lives and environment if—or when—it arrived on their doorsteps?

All witnesses experienced firsthand the opening chapter of a four-year war, one of rapid movement, unexpected developments, and unprecedented violence.

BELGIUM INVADED!

On August 2, Belgium's King Albert (1875–1934) received an official telegram from Germany's government. The diplomatic dispatch claimed that France's army planned to trample through neutral Belgium, using it as a route to invade Germany. The message also argued that the Belgian government should open its borders to German troops for protection. If the Belgian government rejected this offer the country—and its citizens—would be considered Germany's enemies. A reply was due within 12 hours. What was Belgium to do? Its tiny army was no match for Germany's.

Refugees from Belgium in Paris, 1914

"The German army moved into Brussels as smoothly and as compactly as an Empire State express. There were no halts, no open places, no stragglers. . . . All through the night, like a tumult of a river when it races between the cliffs of a canyon, in my sleep I could hear the steady roar of the passing army. And when early in the morning I went to the window the chain of steel was still unbroken. . . . This was a machine, endless, tireless, with the delicate organization of a watch and the brute power of a steam roller. And for three days and three nights through Brussels it roared and rumbled, a cataract of molten lead. The infantry marched singing, with their iron-shod boots beating out the time."

—Richard Harding Davis (1864–1916), reporting on the German army marching through Brussels, Belgium (1914)

Read more of Davis's account at this website. Why is it important to read the reactions of observers of a war, not just the opinions of politicians?

Harding Davis eyewitness

As historian David Olusoga explains, the Western Front was the most diverse place on the planet during World War I. From colonial India alone, England drew between 1.3 and 1.5 million soldiers and laborers. In all, it's estimated that more than 4 million non-white men served in the armies of Europe and the United States.

Watch a video clip about the diversity of the troops.

Olusoga BBC trenches

Germany's "request" for passage was part of a strategy decades in the making, first proposed by Count Alfred von Schlieffen (1833–1913) in the 1870s. The aim was to avoid France's heavily guarded border and invade through the far less fortified country of Belgium. Under German General Helmuth von Moltke the Younger (1848–1916), the attack would be swift. If all went as planned, Belgium would quickly surrender to and cooperate with Germany. Within 39 days, Paris would be captured. France would be out of the war and Germany would re-focus its efforts on the Eastern Front.

But Belgium didn't roll out the red carpet for Germany's troops. Not only did the country reject Germany's request for free passage, it also mobilized its small army, which actively resisted the invasion. Belgian military leaders ordered the destruction of bridges, railroads, tunnels, and dams to halt German progress. The Belgians weren't going to make the march into France an easy one.

The German military had plenty of manpower and firepower, which led to widespread destruction and casualties in Belgium. In towns where resistance was suspected, civilians were used as human shields. In villages across Belgium, residents suspected of sniping at German troops were rounded up and executed.

Terror and looting were part of the strategy to capture Belgium.

In the town of Leuven, suspicion of "illegal civilian resistance" led to the burning of a university library that housed hundreds of thousands of books and included rare Medieval manuscripts. Fire was set to homes and churches. Citizens were shot in the street. Across the country, hostages were taken.

Germans crossing Place Charles Rogier in Belgium, August 20, 1914

Credit: National Museum of the U.S. Navy

These German atrocities—sometimes called "The Rape of Belgium"—sparked global outrage from Ireland and Italy to America and Australia. But outrage alone didn't change the reality that Belgium was officially under German occupation by the end of August 1914. As planned, the occupation of Belgium would be Germany's launching ground for advancing into France.

A BLOODY AUGUST

As German troops marched through Belgium, France set in motion Plan XVII, which hinged on the belief that war would be won by the side that had higher morale and spirit. The thinking went that those with the greater will to win would prove victorious. Under General Joseph Joffre (1852–1913), the French military would march into Alsace-Lorraine, a formerly French territory seized by Germany in the Franco-Prussian War of 1870. On August 7, two French divisions were sent into Alsace. One week later, two more invaded Lorraine.

In the United States, Herbert Hoover (1874–1964) might be best remembered as the president who steered the nation into the Great Depression. But in Belgium, streets and plazas bear his name and he's largely revered as a hero. This is because Hoover spearheaded an effort called the Commission for Relief in Belgium (CRB). When war broke out in 1914, Hoover was working as an engineer in London. He wanted to help those suffering from starvation in Belgium. Through posters and pamphlets, the CRB appealed to U.S. citizens for donations and funds to feed Belgium's refugees. According to historian George Nash, the CRB "was the largest relief operation the world had ever seen to date" and fed more than 9 million people in Belgium for four years, spending nearly $1 billion in relief aid. With its own fleet of ships and flag, the group negotiated treaties with Allied and Central Powers alike.

You can learn more in this article at the National Archives website.

archives Hoover Belgium

But morale was no match against manpower and machine guns. While France predicted that Germany would send 43 units to the Western Front, the country actually sent 83. Outnumbered and out armed, France suffered massive casualties in the first month of the war. On August 22 alone, 27,000 French soldiers died fighting at the Battle of the Frontiers. The recapture of the former French provinces was not going as planned. France was soon in retreat.

MIRACLE OF THE MARNE

Despite Belgian resistance and the arrival of British troops on August 22, Germany advanced into northern France by early September. France's capital, Paris, was in its sights, a mere 25 miles away. Panicked French officials cut telegraph wires and blew up train tracks to sabotage communication and transportation. The government and one-third of Parisians—1 million people—fled the city. Barricades were erected and bridges were lined with explosives in anticipation of the German invasion.

But a stroke of luck on September 2 changed the fortunes of the Allied forces. That afternoon, a French pilot climbed into his ramshackle aircraft made of wood, canvas, glue, and wire and gathered a crucial bit of intelligence from his aerial view—one flank of the German army had changed course. Armed with this information about the repositioning of a unit that was more than 200,000-men strong, the French High Command developed a new tactic for attack.

BATTLE LINES

During the early years of the war, the U.S. government maintained a policy of neutrality. But that didn't keep American citizens from fighting. In 1914, thousands of American men joined the French Foreign Legion. During the war, this division of France's military welcomed more than 35,000 volunteer soldiers from 49 nations into its ranks.

Fighting erupted on September 5 in the farm fields and swampy marshlands around the Marne River. French Commander-in-Chief Joseph Joffre and General Joseph Gallieni (1849–1916), the military governor of Paris, hatched a plan to transport reinforcements to strike the exposed German troops. On September 6, commandeered taxi cabs drove approximately 5,000 French soldiers from the newly formed Sixth Army to the front. Joffre also convinced British General John French (1852–1925) to lend British Expeditionary Forces to the effort. The attack worked, and Germany was forced into retreat.

BATTLE LINES

In total, the French government paid the Parisian drivers who moved troops to the front 70,000 francs for their service. It was the standard rate for transporting two or more passengers beyond the city's limits. After the war, the fleet of taxis and their drivers emerged as symbols of the willingness of all France's people to help in the war effort.

The victory was a surprise to German and Allied forces alike. As one British officer remarked, "Victory, victory . . . when we were so far from expecting it!"

While this win is remembered as the "Miracle of the Marne," it came at a massive human toll. Estimated as the largest battle in history at this point, it included 263,000 Allied casualties. The German military suffered losses in similar numbers. In the months and years that followed, Germany would never come as close to victory again. With the loss at the Marne, some historians even claim that Germany lost more than just a battle—they say the country lost its best chance to win the war.

Read this article on the First Battle of Marne.

Why might myths and legends spring up during times of war?

Smithsonian fleet taxis

DIGGING IN

With losses and fighting on this scale, human resources and critical equipment such as ammunition were in short supply. The power of new weapons, too, made it difficult for either side to advance.

AN AMERICAN AUTHOR IN PARIS RESPONDS

When war erupted in 1914, American author Edith Wharton (1862–1937) was living in Paris. Wharton immediately went to work writing about the war's impact on civilians. She also worked with the French Red Cross to organize relief efforts, including hostels and schools for refugees. According to biographer Julie Olin-Ammentorp, the aid services Wharton established helped more than 9,000 refugees, served more than 235,000 meals, located employment for more than 3,000 refugees, and distributed more than 48,000 articles of clothing.

● ● ● ● ● ●

Because progress was so limited, Allied and Central Powers alike began digging in, creating zigzagging networks of defensive trenches, each 4 feet wide and 6 to 7 feet deep.

The first trenches were dug in September 1914. The technique quickly spread to other battle sites on the Western Front. Soon, more than 400 miles of trenches stretched from the North Sea to the Swiss border, protected by barbed wire and separated by an area labeled "No Man's Land."

Life in the trenches was one of slime and mud. Troops on both sides shared their dirt enclosures with lice, fleas, and rats. On top of the risk from exploding bombs and sharpshooters, illness and disease plagued soldiers.

It was difficult to feed the vast number of men fighting at the front. Many local women were employed for the task.

Credit: Ernst Brooks, National Library of Scotland (CC BY International 4.0)

If conditions were quiet, men served in the trenches for up to 10 days at a time. In periods of wet and cold, troops were rotated out in a four-part cycle, serving on the front line, support line, and reserve line, and then taking a period of rest that allowed for bathing and letter writing.

It was far from the glorious war adventure so many people had imagined in August 1914.

A barber doing his job in a trench in France, 1915

CHRISTMAS TRUCE

Throughout November and December of 1914, rain hammered Western Front troops from above. Machine gun fire and bombs threatened at the surface, and muck sucked at men's feet from below. A freeze on December 24 made movement easier.

BATTLE LINES

Women served in a variety of medical roles on the Western Front. The Scottish Women's Hospital at Royaumont was an effort entirely run by female doctors, nurses, and support staff.

That evening, as author Jim Murphy explains in his book, *Truce: The Day the Soldiers Stopped Fighting*, "In a few places, something remarkable took place. Soldiers from both sides got out of their trenches and cautiously walked into No Man's Land. Meeting in the middle, they would shake hands, exchange cigars or tins of food, and chat. Despite obvious language barriers, a number of these meetings produced promises to continue the peace on Christmas Day."

Listen to an eyewitness to the Christmas truce.

Why do you think the men were happy to engage with soldiers from the other side? Why were people higher in the chain of command angered by the truce?

IWM voices Christmas

ALL'S NOT QUIET ON THE WESTERN FRONT

The *Illustrated London News*'s interpretation of the Christmas truce by A.C. Michael

TEXT TO WORLD

Have you ever stopped a fight for a moment and met with your enemy? How did it make you feel?

On Christmas Day, the truce did continue in many spots. The dead were buried. Gifts were exchanged. Carols were sung, and one German barber offered haircuts to Allied troops. Soccer matches were even reported between the two sides that had—just a day before—been firing at each other.

BATTLE LINES

Adolf Hitler (1889–1945), who was serving on the German side of the trenches, refused to participate in any gestures of goodwill during the Christmas truce.

Not everyone was pleased by the turn of events. Leadership on both sides responded with fury and vowed it would never happen again.

Some soldiers also rejected the temporary peace. English Captain Billy Congreve (1891–1916) remembered, "We have issued orders to the men not on any account to allow a 'truce.' . . . The Germans did try. They came over towards us singing. So we opened rapid fire on them, which is the only truce they deserve."

Still, the Christmas truce represents one of the best-known chapters in World War I, a brief suspension of violence and a moment of recognition of the humanity of those serving on the other side before the fighting began again in earnest.

KEY QUESTIONS

- What impact did the war have on civilians in neutral Belgium and northern France?

- Why was the Battle of the Marne an early turning point in the war?

- Why did troops begin to entrench in late 1914?

THE OTTOMAN EMPIRE

The Ottoman Empire entered the war in November 1914, joining forces with Austria-Hungary and Germany. With 600 years of history behind it, the multiethnic empire had—at its peak—more than 30 million subjects. Its land holdings stretched well into central Europe, with Ottoman forces reaching to Vienna, Austria, in 1529 and 1683. By the early twentieth century, Ottoman leadership faced internal and external threats, such as the threat of revolt from its own provinces and intervention from imperial England, which wanted to ensure routes to colonial India. Why did the Ottoman Empire join forces with the Central Powers? The empire's leader, Enver Pasha (1881–1922), wanted to expand the empire east to include Turkic peoples living under Russian rule. Also, Germany had never tried to annex Ottoman territories, so it seemed a more reliable ally than England or France.

The photo at this website shows the bright red pantaloons donned by French soldiers in the early part of the conflict.

sueddeutsche planten

THE CLOTHES MAKE THE SOLDIER

In 1914, Europe's various militaries could be identified by their uniforms. A French soldier could be easily spotted in his blazing red pantaloons, and a member of Germany's army could be sighted by his spiked "Pickelhaube" hat. In the open fields of the Western Front, these style choices could make men targets for enemy fire. In contrast, other articles of clothing, such as British soldiers' sheepskin jackets, were coveted by enemy troops.

- **Do some research at the library.** You can also watch this video on soldiers' uniforms.

Dan Snow soldier's kit

- **Investigate the evolving military styles of World War I.** Why did some armies enter the war with uniforms poorly suited for battle conditions? How did the uniforms of France, Germany, and England change during the course of the war? Make a timeline that shows how each army's uniforms changed between 1914 and 1918.

- **Consider the following questions.**

  - How and why did certain uniforms make certain troops more of a target than others?

  - Why did certain uniforms not work in the modern war that was World War I?

  - What modifications did various countries make to their uniforms to make them less of a target? Did it work?

  - How did clothing provided by the military better prepare some soldiers for battle than others?

A Pickelhaube hat

Credit: Auckland War Museum (CC BY 2.0)

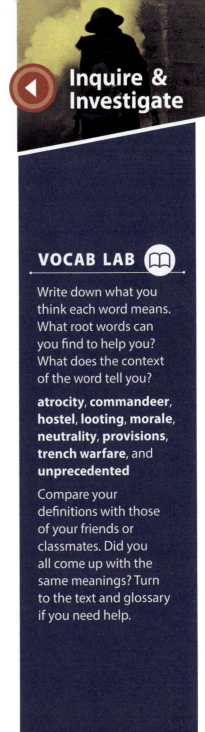

VOCAB LAB

Write down what you think each word means. What root words can you find to help you? What does the context of the word tell you?

atrocity, **commandeer**, **hostel**, **looting**, **morale**, **neutrality**, **provisions**, **trench warfare**, and **unprecedented**

Compare your definitions with those of your friends or classmates. Did you all come up with the same meanings? Turn to the text and glossary if you need help.

To investigate more, consider how military dress continued to change through the twentieth century and into the twenty-first. Look at various wars and conflicts to see how the clothing of soldiers was modified for fighting conditions and new technologies.

THE GEOGRAPHY OF WAR

Belgium is one of Europe's low countries, meaning that much of its land sits below sea level. Through centuries, humans have reshaped and altered the landmass to protect it from the waters of the Atlantic Ocean with a series of seawalls, dams, locks, and dikes. In October 1914, Belgium's King Albert and his government made the deliberate and intentional decision to allow seawater to flood the country in order to halt the German advance to the North Sea.

To investigate more, consider that geography played a strategic role throughout World War I. Research other sites where the landscape impacted the outcome of combat. Places to investigate include the steep and icy Italian Alps, where Italian and Austro-Hungarian troops battled; Mesopotamia, where British and Ottoman forces clashed; or Sarikamish on the Russian front.

• **Research the Battle of the Yser in 1914.**

  • Who was involved in the decision? When and why was it reached?

  • What did they hope to achieve with this decision?

  • How did it impact the German advance?

  • What were the costs of this decision for Belgium? What were its benefits?

• **Study this image and caption that presented the flooding of the Yser to Russian audiences.**

WDL Belgians flooding

  • Who is shown in the print? How are they presented?

  • What does the caption add to understanding of the print?

  • Who do you think this print was produced for and why?

  • Based on what you've learned about the Battle of the Yser, is this image accurate or exaggerated?

Chapter 4 ▶
Old Strategies, New Tech

What were the human costs of new war technologies?

Gas, tanks, U-boats, and other technologically advanced weapons set the stage for new kinds of injuries and ways to die. The landscape and the populations would never be the same.

● ● ● ● ● ● ● ●

Throughout the war, old military strategies gave way to modern weapons. Just a few years earlier, these new technologies would have seemed like the wild imaginings of a mad scientist or science fiction novelist. On land, in the air, and at sea, these instruments of violence allowed combatants to kill and wound each other in numbers never seen before.

Often, the enemy was nameless and faceless, hidden behind a trench wall, soaring overhead in a plane, or encased in a torpedo-firing U-boat. Some of these developments, such as the machine gun, existed before the war. Others, including the tank, were responses to the challenges of trench warfare.

As this war of attrition wore on, each side tried to gain the upper hand through the latest and greatest in technology. These weapons signaled not just the dawn of a new era in warfare—they also represented a totally new modern period of history.

ON LAND

Imagine a dense woodland, stretching as far as the eye can see. Now, imagine this same space just 24 hours later—that forest is completely destroyed. Craters form massive bowls in the earth where trees once stood. Those few trees that still stand are lonely and weak. The leafy ground underfoot has been pummeled into a sticky mud littered with debris and shrapnel. What was once green is now gray, brown, and black. Where life once flourished, it's now totally lifeless.

This was the power of the First World War's shelling and heavy artillery bombardments, which transformed and destroyed landscapes on a colossal scale. So extreme was the destruction that some observers even drew parallels to the ancient Roman city of Pompeii, destroyed by a volcanic eruption during one day in 79 CE. They foresaw future generations visiting these ruins to reflect upon the massive and total ruin of a once-thriving civilization. While European cities were rebuilt and still stand strong, the effect of four years of war is still evident in many places.

> "One really clear way of understanding the shift in World War I in terms of technology is that soldiers rode in on horses and they left in airplanes."
>
> —Historian Libby H. O'Connell

A view of France from the air, 100 years after the end of World War I. You can still see craters and trenches left from the war.

Credit: NASA Earth Observatory image by Lauren Dauphin

Millions of shells fell on the battlefields of World War I. An estimated 20 percent of them didn't explode. Today, these remain hazardous for farmers and residents of Belgium and France, where 40 to 50 tons of shells continue to turn up each year.

To learn more about one man's collection of retrieved shells and other war artifacts on his farm near Ypres, view this video.

Bomb Collector Ypres

From 1915 to 1917, the war on the Western Front became one of attrition. Neither side made any significant advances, because both were powered by weapons that quickly mowed down anyone who dared cross No Man's Land, the area between trench lines. Trenches fenced by barbed wire—often a lethal weapon in itself—were protected by sharpshooting snipers and machine gunners.

As the fighting wore on, generals on both sides resorted to more and more extreme measures, including weapons of mass destruction. Among the earliest of these weapons was poison gas, first used at Ypres, Belgium, in April of 1915.

On April 22, German forces defied the 1907 Hague Convention and unleashed chlorine gas.

While there is a chance this image was staged propaganda, you can see how the landscape was changed by the ongoing bombings.

After a round of heavy shelling ceased, French and French-Algerian colonial troops peered out from their trenches. A yellow-green smog wafted toward them across No Man's Land. The toxin's effects were first felt on the eyes and face. They quickly spread to the throat and lungs, causing victims to choke. These chemical weapons caused the lungs to flood with fluid, essentially drowning a gassed person from the inside-out.

Both sides used gas throughout the war, including the more lethal phosgene and mustard gases. Early on, the methods people had for protecting against gas were very ineffective.

A French soldier with an early type of gas mask

Soldiers were told to hold urine-soaked socks or kerchiefs against their faces for protection. Soon, masks and respirators for humans and horses alike were developed. But even after the air cleared, the potent chemicals lingered in soil and water, coating surfaces like a pollen.

Gases that settled in the soil could even be reactivated if the earth was disturbed.

Western Front soldiers often used dark humor to cope with life in the trenches. After repairing a printing press found in the heavily shelled city of Ypres, members of Great Britain's 12th Battalion, the Sherwood Foresters, even printed a satirical newspaper.

You can read some of it at this website. Why do you think soldiers enjoyed this so much?

NAM Wipers Times

Watch the first use of gas in France and listen to some eyewitness accounts of it in this video.

Why was it such a game changer for the soldiers? How might war outcomes have differed if the Germans had not used gas?

History Germans
first wmd

Soldiers in gas masks

BATTLE LINES

Chemical weapons were often encased in shells hurled at enemy trenches. On impact with a target, the chemical would be airborne. Throughout the war, German forces launched 75,000 tons of poison gas. British and French troops unleashed 56,000 tons. In total, more than 1.2 million soldiers were gas victims, with 91,198 dying from its effects.

By 1916, generals on both sides were willing to make huge sacrifices of human life in order to "bleed" the other side into surrender. German General Erich von Falkenhayn (1861–1922) engineered an offensive attack at Verdun, France, in February of that year.

Germany planned this strategic attack, based on the idea of a meat-grinder strategy, for months.

In von Falkenhayn's view, massive casualties were the only way to win the war.

At Verdun, deep bunkers 40 feet underground were dug and lined with steel and concrete. An extreme bombardment began on February 21. Shelling lasted eight hours and could be heard more than 100 miles away. Then, German forces advanced on Allied lines in units of flame-throwing stormtroopers. But even with such extreme measures and casualties, there was no clear winner. The stalemate continued through the summer and fall, lasting until December.

The Somme offensive was the Allied response to Verdun. While British and French forces pounded German troops with artillery and machine guns, no real progress was made, even though in one instance, 10 British Vickers machine guns fired 1 million rounds continuously for 12 hours. Lasting from July 1 until November 18, the battle was the first in history to result in more than 1 million casualties. At its end, the Allies had captured about 48 square miles, but they hadn't fully broken through German lines.

The challenge of breaking through No Man's Land led to the development of another technology—the combat tank. British engineers began developing armored vehicles to cut through barbed wire in 1915. In the minds of naval leaders such as Winston Churchill (1874–1965), these vehicles would serve as a type of "landship." The armored vehicles quickly evolved into hulking steel machines that led charges across battlefields.

A British tank at the Battle of Flers-Courcelette in the Somme, France, September 15, 1916

Credit: retrieved from Library of Congress

CHINESE LABOUR CORPS

Mechanized warfare resulted in massive death tolls and labor shortages. In 1916, Allied forces began recruiting Chinese laborers to support efforts on the Western Front. Mainly farmers from rural areas, these volunteers risked life and limb to build trenches, lay rail lines, unload essential supplies, bury the dead, and repair machinery. In total, Great Britain's Chinese Labour Corps counted 95,000 workers. Some sources estimate that 20,000 of these men died while serving in France and Belgium.

Chinese visitors and the Chinese Labour Corps

Credit: National Library of Scotland (CC BY 4.0)

UNDERGROUND WAR

Do you think fighting happened only above ground? Think again. Allied and Central Powers both dug tunnels beneath No Man's Land in attempts to attack the other line. On the British side, men who worked as miners in peacetime often labored 12 backbreaking hours a day shoveling these networks. Sometimes, enemy diggers even met and battled underground.

● ● ● ● ● ● ● ●

Check out this map that shows the destructive power of U-boats.

Which year was the worst for naval disasters? Why might that be?

---

storymaps U-boats
WWI

By the later years of the war, tanks paved the way for Allied advances. The Allies had an advantage over German troops in tank production, partially because they established blockades of metals and industrial infrastructure. British and French tanks played a key role during 1918, helping to turn the tide in favor of the Allies.

AT SEA

For centuries, Great Britain held bragging rights as the world's greatest sea power. England's naval strength allowed it to build an expansive empire that stretched across continents and oceans. In 1913, 23 percent of the world's population lived under British rule. The Union Jack flew over cities in India and South Africa and in coastal towns in Australia and Jamaica.

Because of the human and natural resources that these colonies and dominions provided, England developed into an industrial and economic superpower.

When Germany began to rise as a global force in the late nineteenth century, challenging England's naval status became a priority. An arms race was on to build the most powerful and most modern fleet of ships. When England began constructing state-of-the-art battleships known as dreadnoughts in the early 1900s, Germany responded by doing the same.

From the outset of war, the fight to control the high seas was most evident in the endless battle between stealthy German submarines and above-water ships and merchant vessels. Great Britain used its naval fleet to blockade German ports. This meant that critical materials needed for Germany's military and civilian populations couldn't be imported.

Germany responded by targeting both the British fleet and neutral ships carrying supplies to England and France. German forces used torpedo-shooting submarines, or U-boats, to do this.

During the four years of war, U-boat torpedoes sank a total of 5,554 merchant and warships. The most famous of these, the passenger ship the RMS *Lusitania*, was struck by a torpedo on May 7, 1915, off the coast of Ireland. It sank in less than 20 minutes, largely because of the explosive munitions it was secretly transporting. The tragedy resulted in 1,201 deaths—128 of them American—and swung American public opinion about the war.

An undated photo of the RMS *Lusitania*, taken between 1907 and 1913

Credit: George Grantham Bain

While Germany and England each possessed a full fleet of warships a decade in the making, these powerful vessels faced off just once during the war. In 1916, the rival forces met in the Battle of Jutland, just off the coast of Denmark. Each side came to the battle equipped with guns that could hurl massive shells at targets up to 18 miles away. After several ships on both sides were sunk, both fleets retreated. No clear winner emerged from this North Sea engagement.

DESIGN THINKING

How could the Allies stop German U-boats from torpedoing ships?
Many ideas were proposed, from covering ships with mirrors to making vessels look like whales or islands. The concept that actually worked was inspired by zebras. British zoologist John Graham Kerr (1869–1957) proposed using disrupting camouflage to disguise ships. Great Britain's navy rejected the idea. But in 1917, it was picked up by artist and ship painter Norman Wilkinson, who suggested that ships be painted in fragmented, bright colors that made them look broken apart. The strategy worked. In the United States and Great Britain, thousands of people set to work painting more than 2,700 ships and convoy escorts. In the coming years, this even inspired fashion trends!

● ● ● ● ● ● ● ● ● ●

BY AIR

Just 11 years before the first shots of World War I rang out, the Wright Brothers defied gravity and lifted off in flight. Given the newness of aviation, this was the first major conflict in which it was tested.

As one historian notes, "Everything about using aircraft in war was invented in World War I."

Soon into the war, pilots came to be embraced as the "eyes of the army" from above. From the skies, planes on the Eastern and Western Fronts alike gathered critical intelligence and dropped bombs on enemy targets. Allied and Central Power reconnaissance pilots often passed each other in the air as they crossed lines to spy on the ground below.

Soon, attempts to shoot down spy planes, first with handheld pistols and later with mounted machine guns, became a priority. By 1916, airborne dogfights were happening thousands of feet above the ground, with teams of ace fliers competing to send the other side's crafts plunging to the ground.

Because of the danger of combat piloting and the newness of aviation, airborne units were celebrated by the likes of British Prime Minister David Lloyd George (1863–1945) as "the knighthood of the war." Those who did survive combat, such as Germany's Manfred von Richthofen (1892–1918), also known as the "Red Baron," gained global attention for their airborne antics.

BATTLE LINES

Warring groups didn't use just people and machines in battle. They also brought animal allies to the conflict. Horses and dogs—which served in cavalry charges and as transportation and messengers—are among the most recognized animal faces of World War I. But other, more unusual animals also served.

Slugs: Used by American troops to detect mustard gas, they sense the chemical and show signs of distress before humans.

Sea lions: British forces tried to train sea lions to locate U-boats and pop to the surface to indicate their location.

Birds: Carrier pigeons were used by the Allies to relay messages when communication systems were unreliable. Central Power forces trained hawks to attack and intercept these pigeons.

Glow worms: Allied troops often used bioluminescent glow worms to read battle plans and letters in the trenches.

Handley-Page two-engined bomber in flight over oil tanks. The outbreak of World War I led to this design of the first two-engine bomber.

Credit: U.S. Air Force

The weapons of World War I killed more than 9 million soldiers and wounded an additional 21 million.

The toll wasn't just physical, it was also mental. Extreme fighting conditions drove millions of soldiers to the point of psychological breakdown. Millions developed what was known at the time as shellshock, a term coined just six months into the war. Symptoms ranged from uncontrollable movement, such as chronic shaking and facial tics, to extreme anxiety, nightmares, and hallucinations.

BATTLE LINES

The average life expectancy of an Allied pilot in April 1916 was just 11 days.

Treatments included rest, hypnosis, and electroshock therapy. Despite the high numbers of men presenting with psychological distress, the British War Office Committee rejected the diagnosis of shellshock in 1922.

AIRSHIPS

Massive balloon airships, known in German as zeppelins, were used by both sides during the war. Like planes, these crafts were used to gather intelligence over land and at sea. They were also used to drop bombs. During the war's four years, British cities saw 51 airship attacks, which killed 557 people and wounded 1,358. However, advances in aviation literally deflated the power of the airship—as planes flew ever-higher, these giant balloons were easily shot down by enemy pilots.

Write down what you think each word means. What root words can you find to help you? What does the context of the word tell you?

attrition, **dreadnought**, **reconnaissance**, **respirator**, **shellshock**, **shrapnel**, **sparring**, **U-boats**, and **zeppelins**

Compare your definitions with those of your friends or classmates. Did you all come up with the same meanings? Turn to the text and glossary if you need help.

In WWI, Indian troops of the British Empire who were wounded on the Western Front were hospitalized in the Royal Pavilion in Brighton, England. The Hindu soldiers who died were cremated at this site overlooking the city, which is now known as the Chattri memorial.

Each and every one of these casualties had a ripple effect on the lives of loved ones in places ranging from New Zealand to Turkey to Senegal to Morocco. Towns in England lost entire generations of young, male residents. People lost brothers, sons, fathers, and friends in the race to "bleed" the other side. In these many individuals across the planet, the loss was felt for generations.

TEXT TO WORLD

What technology has changed in your lifetime? How has it affected you?

KEY QUESTIONS

- **How did military technology change from the beginning to the end of World War I?**

- **Why did these new technologies lead to widespread casualties and destruction?**

DESCRIBING THE INDESCRIBABLE

Throughout and well after World War I, poets, journalists, and soldiers alike tried to find words to capture the horror and scale of destruction. Often, they relied on metaphor, simile, and personification to relay what they witnessed to audiences on the home front.

- **Research these types of speech.** What are metaphors and similes? What is personification? How are they similar and different? Write an example of each.

- **Analyze the following primary source passages.** In each, identify what figurative device the author uses. Who is the author? When and where were they writing? What do they describe? In your view, how effective is their use of language?

"The cloud of smoke advanced like a yellow low wall, overcoming all those who breathed in poisonous fumes."
—*The Daily Mail* (United Kingdom), April 26, 1914

"We heard strange throbbing noises, and lumbering slowly towards us came three huge mechanical monsters such as we had never seen before. My first impression was that they looked ready to topple on their noses, but their tails and the two-little wheels at the back held them down and kept them level."
—British signal officer Bert Cheney, September 1916

"It was like mowing grass, only the grass grew up as fast as you mowed it. . . . Every time the sergeant yelled, 'Feu!' I got sicker and sicker. They had wives and children, hadn't they?"
—American machine gunner Eugene Bullard (1895–1961), who fought alongside French troops at Verdun, 1916

To investigate more, think of all the poets and war witnesses on all sides of the conflict who processed their experiences in verse. Visit the Poetry Foundation's website to read a selection of poems about the war. Then, craft your own poem about the war.

Poetry Foundation WWI

THE TIN MASKS OF WAR

The casualties of war included not just those who died on the battlefields and in the trenches. It also included those who returned home, often with disfiguring injuries. The weapons of World War I claimed entire parts of soldiers' faces—eyes, ears, noses, and chins could all be cruelly taken by shrapnel and bullets. Men were often so disturbed by their own unrecognizable faces that mirrors were banned in many recovery wards.

* **Research the wartime work of sculptors Francis Derwent Wood and Anna Coleman Ladd and plastic surgeon Sir Harold Gillies.** Head to the library or try these online resources.

  * Who were they treating?

  * Where were they working?

  * What were the nature of the injuries they addressed?

  * How did they use their skills to help wounded soldiers?

* **Think about these injuries as a result of the weapons and combat conditions of World War I.** What technological changes led to this huge number of patients with severe facial disfigurement? Write a paragraph summarizing how technology and fighting conditions created a generation of permanently wounded men.

NPR masks
soldiers

Smithsonian
faces war

NAM plastic
surgery

To investigate more, think of the countless other scientists who applied their knowledge and skills to aid the battle wounded. One of them was Nobel Prize-winning chemist and physicist Marie Curie (1867–1934). Research her use of X-rays during World War I to learn how this technology also helped save lives.

Chapter 5

The Eastern Front and Revolution in Russia

THE WAR DID NOT TAKE A TOLL ON JUST THE SOLDIERS. IT CAUSED UNREST OFF THE BATTLEFIELD AS WELL.

Bread Line

How were social and political revolutions a part of WWI?

As the war dragged on, various countries were confronted with the problem of rebellion and revolution among their own people. Russia in particular found it impossible to continue to fight while the country's population was in a state of turmoil.

With the largest population in Europe, the Russian Empire had no lack of fighting forces. Its military, however, had suffered from a chronic shortage of weapons and weak communications since the early months of the war. By the middle years of the war, this led to millions of disillusioned soldiers and civilians alike—and the stirrings of revolution.

Doubt and unease about the war's progress wasn't just an issue in Russia—all across Europe, war-weariness set in by 1916.

Not only did this doubt and unease raise the possibility of revolution, it also created room for scapegoats, or communities blamed and persecuted for any and all problems. In Russia and the Ottoman Empire, this meant that Jewish and Armenian minorities suffered tragic fates.

A MOBILIZED GIANT

On August 17, 1914, the Russian army went on the offensive and marched into Germany. During these opening battles, Russia's sheer manpower caught the German military off guard. With troops now on two fronts, Germany needed to quickly identify the weaknesses of their Eastern Front enemy. They found it in Russia's communications systems. Russia's high command was transmitting uncoded messages about the war. This allowed German authorities to pinpoint the exact who, what, when, where, and how of Russian plans.

On August 31, Germany's military applied that intercepted intelligence. Under the leadership of Paul von Hindenburg (1847–1934) and Erich Ludendorff (1865–1937), German forces encircled Russian troops at Tannenberg and forced a surrender. In this battle alone, 80,000 Russian soldiers were killed. An additional 100,000 men were captured, along with already scarce artillery.

BATTLE LINES

The Eastern Front stretched across 900 miles, from the grassy flatlands of Russia's steppes to the peaks of the Ural Mountains.

Despite widespread anti-Semitism, between 500,000 and 650,000 Jewish men served in the Russian army during World War I. The German army also had a significant force of 100,000 Jewish conscripts, 12,000 of whom were killed and 30,000 of whom received military honors.

• • • • • • • • • •

A German soldier

Credit: National Library of Scotland (CC BY 4.0)

PALE OF SETTLEMENT

Before and during World War I, the majority of Russia's 4 million Jews were forced to live in what was called the "Pale of Settlement." This area includes modern-day Belarus, Lithuania, and Moldova, as well as parts of Ukraine, Latvia, Poland, and Russia. In the Pale, Professor Monika Richarz notes, "Most Jews lived in great poverty, crammed into towns . . . . Many of them had no jobs at all and relied on alms." Russia's persecution of its Jewish population and other minority groups through organized pogroms pushed migration in droves.

Between 1900 and 1914, more than 2 million people fled to begin new lives in the United States. How do you think people felt when they left their home country?

● ● ● ● ● ● ● ●

These events were basically repeated in September. At the Battle of Masurian Lakes, Russia lost another 100,000 soldiers. With superior technology and better-equipped troops, Germany tipped the balance of power in their favor just a few weeks into the war.

Russian female nurses and hospital orderlies interact with male counterparts.

Elsewhere on the Eastern Front, Russia squared off against the other Central Powers. For six months, beginning in September 1914, Russian troops besieged the Austro-Hungarian fortressed city of Przemyśl, pushing residents to starvation. Forces lobbed shells inside the city's walls, waiting for the people to surrender.

With a population that reflected the diversity of the Austro-Hungarian Empire as a whole—including Slavic and Jewish groups—mistrust and suspicions simmered. Austrian authorities went so far as to hang citizens suspected of sympathizing with Russia.

In March 1915, after 133 days, Przemyśl finally fell. Invading Russian forces attacked Jewish residents, who made up one-third of the city's population. These were anti-Semitic attacks, driven by the misconception that Jewish people were to blame for the wrongs of the world. Observer Helena Jabłońska (1864–1936) watched as soldiers "waited until the Jews set off to the synagogue for their prayers before setting upon them with whips. They were deaf to any pleas for mercy, regardless of age." These actions were consistent with the policies of Imperial Russia, which encouraged segregation and persecution of its Jewish minority.

In the middle of the siege of Przemyśl, in a battle that erupted in December 1914, Russia clashed with the war's newest entrant, the Ottoman Empire. Fighting broke out in rugged mountains near the town of Sarikamish in the Caucasus. Sub-zero temperatures, ice, and snow plagued troops, hitting Turkish forces, who were unequipped for the brutal cold, especially hard.

A combination of poor leadership and harsh conditions led to the worst Ottoman loss of the war.

Learn more about the Armenian genocide in this video.

Caution: This video contains disturbing imagery

How do these events fit into the larger puzzle of World War I?

Facing History Armenian Genocide

Ottoman atrocities against the Armenians were well-documented throughout the war. A massive refugee relief effort was launched in the United States in response to the crisis.

GIVE OR WE PERISH

AMERICAN COMMITTEE FOR RELIEF IN THE NEAR EAST

ARMENIA – GREECE – SYRIA – PERSIA

CAMPAIGN for $30,000,000

THE HAMIDIAN MASSACRES

The genocide of 1915–1918 wasn't the first time that Armenians in the Ottoman Empire had been targeted by authorities. Armenian efforts to gain political rights in the 1890s were brutally suppressed by Sultan Abdul Hamid II (1842–1918), who sought total elimination of minority protest and dissent. An estimated 200,000 Armenians lost their lives between 1894 and 1896 in what were labeled the Hamidian massacres.

● ● ● ● ● ● ● ●

Official records report more than 60,000 casualties, with 33,000 killed. Many of those who died froze to death. The Ottoman government shifted the blame onto Armenian soldiers, claiming treachery within their ranks. The military then disarmed and dismissed these soldiers to labor camps, where maltreatment led to starvation, disease, and often death.

Many were systematically murdered. They were among the first casualties of the Armenian genocide.

THE ARMENIAN GENOCIDE

In 1914, Christian Armenians lived in provinces of both the Russian and Ottoman Empires. An ethnic and religious minority in Ottoman lands, authorities had long regarded their 2 million Christian Armenian subjects with suspicion. While Armenian and other minority groups in the Ottoman Empire gained some rights after a change in rule in 1908, a fringe element seized power in October 1913.

These radicals preached the idea of Turkey for the Turks, which gained traction after the massive losses of territory in the Balkan Wars. Minority groups had no place in this vision.

After the Ottoman losses in the winter of 1914–1915, Armenian soldiers were scapegoated as subversives. By spring 1915, the push to purge Anatolia of its Armenian population spread beyond the military. In late April, Armenian intellectuals and community leaders in Constantinople were targeted for imprisonment, torture, and execution. Then, able-bodied, young Armenian men were segregated, rounded up, and deported outside of the city, where butcher squads awaited.

L'AVANCE DES FORCES ALLIÉES AUX DARDANELLES DURANT LA PREMIÈRE QUINZAINE DE MAI

General plan of the Anglo-French attack on the Dardanelles.
Map published April 16, 1915, by the *Weekly Mirror*.

MORE DOMINOES

Smaller countries such as Italy and Bulgaria watched the first months of World War I unfold, weighing which side to join. Italian troops sided with the Allies and engaged in extreme, high-altitude combat against Austro-Hungarian forces in the Alps. Bulgaria aligned itself with the Central Powers. Together with Germany and Austria-Hungary, Bulgaria's military seized control of Serbia in 1915, leading to a massive refugee crisis. How does this show that WWI was truly a global conflict?

Village by village, orders for the "relocation" of all other Armenians—women, children, and the elderly—were issued later in the year. These Armenian civilians were forced to march south in caravans to camps in the remote Syrian desert. These marches were intended to drive people to starvation and exhaustion, and people died by the thousands.

In total, the genocide claimed an estimated 1.5 million lives between 1915 and 1918. Can you think of any other time when a minority was forced to march to relocate, resulting in many deaths?

BATTLE LINES

Despite countless eyewitness accounts and survivor testimonies, the government of Turkey still refuses to acknowledge the Armenian genocide. Why do you think this is the case?

YOU SAY YOU WANT A REVOLUTION?

The threat of revolution wasn't limited to Russia. By 1916, the war's economic and social stresses led to strikes, riots, and mutinies across Europe. In March 1916, workers in England and Scotland took to the streets by the hundreds of thousands to press for better wages and working conditions. In France, Austria, and Germany, riots—often led by women—over food shortages and soaring prices became regular occurrences. French troops mutinied in the spring and summer of 1917, with massive numbers of infantry men abandoning the line in protest of poor food and leave policies.

● ● ● ● ● ● ●

A THIRD FRONT?

As stalemates and casualty counts rose on all fronts, the promises of summer 1914, such as soldiers would be home to witness autumn's changing leaves, or, at the very least, to enjoy holiday festivities, seemed distant and cruel. The military masterminds of both the Allied and Central Powers sought a breakthrough—all sides wanted to open a third front.

Great Britain and France's first big plan was for a coordinated attack on the Strait of Dardanelles, which connects the Mediterranean and Black Seas. The Allied Powers chose this site for several reasons.

It was Ottoman land, and seizing it would likely knock Turkish forces out of the war. It would also allow them to funnel supplies and manpower to and from Russia, their other major ally. Great Britain could flex its naval might in the process and might also gain a foothold in the oil-rich region. The Gallipoli campaign of 1915 was born.

BATTLE LINES

In 1914, St. Petersburg, Russia, was renamed Petrograd. The change was made because St. Petersburg was thought to be too Germanic. The British royal family also changed its name during the war: In 1917, the German-sounding House of Saxe-Coburg and Gotha became the more English House of Windsor.

Far from the breakthrough that the Allies desired, Gallipoli was a nearly year-long disaster that claimed 46,000 lives. Turkish forces were better-prepared and better-equipped than the Allies anticipated and were fighting on familiar ground. Trench warfare quickly took hold. As casualties mounted, so, too, did illness, spread by black corpse flies. The campaign ended with a humiliating Allied retreat in January 1916.

The quest for a third front didn't stop at the Dardanelles. Allied and Central Powers both instigated fighting in colonies on the African continent, across the Middle East, and in China and the Pacific. Germany initiated naval faceoffs on the high seas, near the British colonies of the Falkland Islands and India.

The strategy was to attack Britain's vast empire and force England to defend its far-flung territories.

The aim was always to divert troops, supplies, and resources to places other than the war's two main fronts, the Eastern and Western Fronts. Plus, Great Britain promised Bedouin groups in the Arabian Peninsula independence if they rose up against the Ottoman Empire. The Bedouin soldiers kept their word in the 1916 Arab Revolt. The British and the French, however, did not—they instead planned to partition the area after the war in their favor.

The title reads, "Political demonstration of the 18th of June, 1917, at Petrograd." The left banner reads, "All power to the people - peace to the whole world - all land to the people." The right banner reads, "Down with the minister-capitalists." These were Bolshevik slogans.

THE EASTER REBELLION

With British troops occupied overseas, Irish revolutionaries seized the moment to pursue independence from England. The rebels counted on support from Germany, which sought to destabilize Great Britain's colonies. The pinnacle of this effort was the Easter Rebellion. In April 1916, 1,600 nationalists occupied key points across Dublin. While the uprising was quickly suppressed and lacked popular support, the harsh death sentences issued to rebel leaders sparked outrage—and broader support for an independent Ireland.

The remains of the General Post Office on Sackville Street (later O'Connell Street), Dublin, in the aftermath of the 1916 Rising.
Credit: National Library of Ireland

BLOODY SUNDAY

Russia was no stranger to uprisings caused by frustration with war. In 1905, Russia's failure in the Russo-Japanese War led to organized protest. Workers, peasants, and members of the military numbering 140,000 marched on the Winter Palace, the official residence of Russia's royal family, to present a petition for reforms. The tsar issued the order to fire on the crowd, leaving more than 1,000 dead. Remembered as "Bloody Sunday," it cemented Nicholas II's reputation as a brutal autocrat.

● ● ● ● ● ● ● ● ●

BATTLE LINES

Bolshevik leader Vladimir Lenin (1870–1924) was living in exile in Zurich during the March Revolution of 1917. His return to Russia by train was engineered by German foreign minister Arthur Zimmermann (1864–1940). Zimmermann and others in the German government helped because they thought that the collapse of the tsar's regime and the rise of the Bolsheviks would spell an end to Russia's participation in the war.

REVOLUTION IN RUSSIA

Tsar Nicholas II received an urgent message from the president of Russia's legislative body on March 11, 1917.

"The situation is serious. The capital is in a state of anarchy. The government is paralyzed. Transport service and the supply of food and fuel are completely disrupted. General discontent is growing. There is wild shooting in the streets. In places troops are firing at each other. It is necessary that some person who enjoys the confidence of the country be entrusted immediately with the formation of a new government. There can be no delay. Any procrastination is tantamount to death."

As commander-in-chief of the military, Nicholas was far from the capital, Petrograd, when protests erupted on March 8. It was International Women's Day, and the activists—largely female factory workers—gathered to protest food shortages and endless breadlines. Their actions sparked a revolution, with more than 100,000 workers joining their strike by the day's end. The calls of "Down with hunger!" "Bread for the workers!" "Down with the war!" and "Down with the tsar!" echoed across the city.

By March 10, the number of protesters reached 300,000. The next day, Petrograd's police force tried to regain control by firing on demonstrators. Protestors reacted with panic and stampedes.

The military was instructed to back the police and maintain control of the crowd. But many of these war-weary soldiers were sympathetic with the activists and refused to shoot. They abandoned their posts in droves and joined the cause of revolution.

Less than a week after the women's march, protesters had gained control of the city's streets. Nicholas finally recognized the seriousness of the threat posed to his monarchy and climbed aboard a train to return to Petrograd.

Members of the legislature urged him to abdicate the throne to prevent the disorder from spreading to soldiers on the front. Nicholas consented and passed control to his brother, Michael, who refused the throne. This meant that 300 years of Romanov reign in Russia had ended. Power now rested in the hands of a provisional government headed by the moderate socialist, Alexander Kerensky (1881–1970).

The provisional government had competition for power in the Petrograd Soviet of Workers' and Soldiers' Deputies, a group that represented the interests of workers and the military. It served as a sort of second government that often challenged the official government.

While the official government wanted to continue the war, the Soviets promised to end it.

Mistrustful of politicians, the Soviets were led by activists who promised power to the workers and "peace, land, and bread." These two groups struggled with each other to govern until November 1917, when Bolshevik revolutionaries led by Vladimir Lenin and Leon Trotsky (1879–1940) seized power.

WOMEN'S BATTALION OF DEATH

Russia's provisional government was determined to win the war. In May 1917, a group of militant female soldiers partnered with leaders to take up arms and continue the fight. Formed and led by 25-year-old soldier Maria Bochkareva (1889–1920), the Women's Battalion of Death wanted not just to draw new female cadets, but also to shame men into service. Approximately 2,000 women joined the force. As historian Adam Hochschild describes, these warrior women, "shaved their heads, slept on bare boards during training, endured the same corporal punishment as male Russian soldiers, and sported a skull-and-crossbones insignia."

BOLSHEVIKS OPT OUT OF WAR

Bolshevik leaders promised an end to war, and sought to make good on it. In December 1917, Germany agreed to discuss an armistice agreement. Early peace talks were unsuccessful and fighting resumed at the Eastern Front in early 1918. But on March 3, the Treaty of Brest-Litovsk was signed by representatives from both countries, ending Russia's participation in World War I.

The terms of the treaty provided independence to Ukraine, Georgia, and Finland. It also ceded Poland, the Baltic states, and parts of the Caucasus to the Central Powers.

But signing a treaty didn't spell peace for Russia and its people. Instead, civil war plagued the country through 1922. Bolsheviks, anti-Communist monarchists, and nationalist armies of independence-seekers collided.

It was the costliest civil war in history, claiming between 7 and 12 million combatant and civilian lives. Among the casualties were former Tsar Nicholas II and his family, who were executed while under house arrest in July 1918.

VOCAB LAB

Write down what you think each word means. What root words can you find to help you? What does the context of the word tell you?

abdicate, **anarchy**, **Bolshevik**, **caravan**, **chronic**, **disillusioned**, **persecute**, **pogrom**, **scapegoat**, and **subversive**

Compare your definitions with those of your friends or classmates. Did you all come up with the same meanings? Turn to the text and glossary if you need help.

TEXT TO WORLD

Have you ever witnessed or been a part of a march for social change? What does a revolution make you think of in terms of history?

KEY QUESTIONS

• How was fighting different on the Eastern and Western Fronts?

• How does the Armenian genocide relate to World War I?

• Why did the Allies want to open a third front? How might the war have been different if they'd stuck to two fronts?

EYEWITNESS ACCOUNTS

The crimes committed against the Armenians were well-documented—*The New York Times* ran 145 articles on the atrocities in 1915 alone—and caused widespread global outrage.

- **Examine the following eyewitness accounts of the Armenian genocide.** Consider these questions.

  - Who created these primary sources? When and where were they created?

  - What does the account show or tell about the genocide?

  - How did the creator come to gather this information?

- **Analyze the effects of these sources on people at the time.**

  - How did the general public in the United States respond to reports of genocide in Armenia?

- **Consider researching the Near East Relief Committee.** This is an American humanitarian organization created to aid Armenian refugees.

Armin T. Wegner photographs

"500 Thousand Armenians Said to Have Perished," *The New York Times*, September 24, 1915

"Armenian Massacres: Turkey's Extermination Policies," *The Glasgow Herald*, September 25, 1915

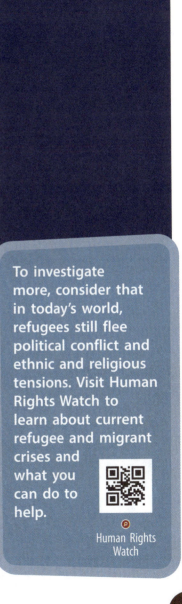

To investigate more, consider that in today's world, refugees still flee political conflict and ethnic and religious tensions. Visit Human Rights Watch to learn about current refugee and migrant crises and what you can do to help.

Human Rights Watch

WHAT IS COMMUNISM?

Karl Marx (1818–1883) and Friedrich Engels (1820–1895) introduced the idea of communism to the world in 1848. This influential political and economic ideology gained supporters worldwide—including Russia's Bolsheviks—who aimed to put this theory into practice.

- **Head to the library or use the internet to research Marx and Engels and answer the following questions.**

  - What is the central conflict they identified in societies?

  - What kind of social, economic, and political systems did they advocate? Why?

  - How did they propose bringing about this change?

- **Then, research the Bolshevik Revolution and the Communist government it created in Russia.**

  - Who were the leaders of this movement?

  - What changes did the Bolsheviks want?

  - How did they achieve them?

  - Was there space for dissent or disagreement under this form of government?

- **Compare Marx and Engels's arguments with the practices of Bolshevik Communists.** Were the policies the Bolsheviks put in place consistent with Marx and Engels's ideas? In your view, would Marx and Engels have considered this revolution a success?

To investigate more, know that communism often gets confused with socialism. Research further to identify the differences between the two related-yet-distinct systems of governance. Then, pinpoint countries in our world today that operate under these systems.

Chapter 6

Neutral
No Longer

How did American
citizens feel about
the entry of the
United States into
World War I?

After several years of neutrality, the United States entered the fray in 1917. As soldiers began to train and the home front began to hum with activity, different groups in the country remained divided on the question of whether joining the war was the right decision.

● ● ● ● ● ● ● ●

On April 2, 1917, U.S. President Woodrow Wilson (1856–1924) stood before a joint session of the U.S. Congress. In a 36-minute speech, he made the case for something that he'd sought to avoid for nearly three years—war with Germany. It was a leap for a president who had won reelection just a few months earlier on the unofficial slogan, "He kept us out of war." It was a leap for a president who, in January 1917, sought to broker a "peace without victory."

But now, Wilson argued before his peers that, "The world must be made safe for democracy." In his words, the German government was a "natural foe of liberty." Four days later, Congress approved a resolution in favor of war.

Neutral no longer, the United States now allied itself with France, Great Britain, and Russia.

In the year and a half that followed, more than 2 million American soldiers from all backgrounds and regions of the country would find themselves fighting on the other side of the Atlantic. And on the home front, as suspicions of disloyal "others" ran high, German-Americans and those opposed to war found themselves targeted for their ethnicity and political beliefs by neighbors and legislation alike.

What happened between January and April 1917 that steered the United States away from an official policy of neutrality and into Europe's trenches? How would this decision reshape American life—at home and on the global stage—in the short and long term?

Read President Wilson's speech at this website. In it he says, "The question upon which the whole future peace and policy of the world depends is this: Is the present war a struggle for a just and secure peace or only for a new balance of power?"

What do you think he means?

President Wilson peace without victory

In 1918, one out of every three U.S. residents were either born abroad or were a first-generation American. New York's Ellis Island was a common port of arrival for European immigrants in the early twentieth century. On the West Coast, Angel Island in San Francisco, California, served as the disembarking site for immigrants from 82 nations.

Credit: Lewis Hine, 1905

A POLICY OF NEUTRALITY

Just more than 120 years before Wilson's war request, George Washington (1732–1799) had issued his farewell address. In the document, America's first president warned against U.S. involvement in the politics of Europe. Washington's words impacted more than a century of American thinking on foreign policy, inspiring isolationist approaches toward political events on the other side of the Atlantic.

When war broke out in 1914, the Wilson administration kept with this tradition, maintaining a policy of neutrality. The majority of Americans supported this position. Neutrality made sense socially, politically, militarily, and economically. Socially and politically, the United States was a diverse melting pot, with immigrants from nations on all sides of the conflict. For politicians, choosing a side meant potentially alienating voters.

Militarily, the United States was weak—its small standing army was far from prepared for combat.

Neutrality was also profitable. When the war began, the U.S. economy was in recession. With farm and factory laborers deployed to the battlefields, European countries—particularly England and France—relied on the United States for food and supplies. U.S. exports jumped from $2.3 billion in 1913 to $4.3 billion in 1916 to a whopping $6.3 billion in 1917. Bankers also profited from lending massive sums of money to the Allied Powers. In the course of four years, the war transformed the United States into the world's major financial power.

BATTLE LINES

On August 29, 1914, pacifist women paraded down New York City's Fifth Avenue. Planned as a "mourning" parade, the women marched from 58th Street to Union Square as if in a funeral procession. As New York's *Evening World* newspaper reported, "Every woman in the slow-moving line wore some badge of mourning . . . as a token of the black death which is hovering over the European battlefields."

But not all Americans were neutral about the war. Fierce anti- and pro-war groups also used their voices—on the streets and in the popular press—to express a split from the government's position.

For example, the pacifist Woman's Peace Party (WPP) was formed in response to the war and numbered 40,000 members at its peak. A statement issued on its formation in January 1915 illustrates the organization's purpose: "We women of the United States, assembled in behalf of World Peace, grateful for the security of our own country, but sorrowing for the misery of all involved in the present struggle among warring nations, do hereby band ourselves together to demand that war be abolished."

The WPP pushed for limiting arms, peaceful resolution to the war in Europe, and eliminating the economic causes of war. This diverse coalition included advocates who had gained organizing experience in the women's suffrage and temperance movements.

The Women's Peace Parade, 1914

On the other side of the coin were war hawks, who sought a new era of American intervention in global affairs. Leading the charge? Former U.S. President Theodore Roosevelt (1858–1919).

So eager was Roosevelt to enter the fight, he even petitioned Wilson to let him form and lead his own volunteer army.

A movement for preparedness gained traction from late 1914 onward. Armed with similar strategies to anti-war forces, war preppers also organized parades, wrote scathing editorials, and lobbied politicians to adopt their position. Popular summer training camps even emerged to ready young men for possible combat. At $100, the 35-day course was largely reserved for the sons of wealthy elites. Once America entered the war, its curriculum was adapted as the basic training provided to all new soldiers.

TIPPING POINTS

What tipped the United States from a neutral country to a combatant nation? Even during the early months of 1917, the Wilson administration hoped to broker a peace. But a string of events shattered the country's isolationist line.

"The peoples of every land are longing for the time when love shall conquer hate, when co-operation shall replace conflict, when war shall be no more."

—The Friends National Peace Committee, March 20, 1917

● ● ● ● ● ● ●

Early in the war, a German U-boat sank the passenger liner the RMS *Lusitania*, killing more than 1,000 people. Public outrage over the demise of the *Lusitania* and an unarmed French ship in 1916 led Germany to avoid attacking ships that didn't belong to its direct enemies. But by early 1917, the effect of England's naval blockade on German food supplies was taking a major toll.

Americans arrive at the front

Credit: Ernest Brooks, National Library of Scotland (CC BY International 4.0)

In early February, Germany resumed its policy of considering neutral and passenger vessels to be fair targets. Just weeks after Wilson issued his plea for "peace without victory," Germany announced that its submarines would no longer spare neutral or passenger vessels on the high seas. The logic was the same as that of the blockade—the U-boats would prevent ships carrying food and critical supplies from reaching England's shores. Great Britain would be starved into surrender.

With U.S. lives at risk, the Wilson administration cut diplomatic ties with Germany's government. Later in February, the decision was reached to arm merchant vessels. And although ships traveled in convoys and were dazzle-painted to camouflage with the moving sea, U-boats still managed to sink 423 merchant and neutral vessels in April 1917.

View this video to learn more about how Germany's policy of unrestricted submarine warfare pulled the United States into World War I.

#USWW100
unrestricted submarine

BATTLE LINES

Germany's fleet of 140 subs had destroyed about 30 percent of the world's merchant vessels by 1917, sending millions of tons of cargo to the ocean floor.

JEANNETTE RANKIN

In the world of politics, Jeannette Rankin (1880–1973) was notable among the war's dissenters. From Montana, Rankin was the first woman elected to the U.S. Congress. The year was 1916, four full years before women could even vote. She was sworn in on April 2, 1917. Later that evening, President Wilson issued his address to Congress advocating for the United States's entry into war. Rankin had long been a pacifist. Four days later, when the first vote was called, she abstained. On the second vote, she rose and said, "I want to stand by my country, but I cannot vote for war." Although 49 other members of the body also voted "nay," the resolution passed. The country was at war.

A second shock wave rattled the United States in March 1917—the release of the Zimmermann telegram. It was sent from Germany's foreign minister to the government of Mexico, where the United States had recently engaged in border skirmishes with revolutionary forces.

The telegram proposed that if the United States entered the war on the Allied side, Mexico and Germany should "make war together," and "make peace together." It promised "generous financial support and an understanding on our part that Mexico is to reconquer the lost territory in Texas, New Mexico, and Arizona."

These factors were enough to sway public opinion, and the president, in the direction of war.

A Red Cross outpost, 1918. During World War I, American soldiers were commonly referred to as "doughboys." No one knows the exact origins of the nickname. British troops were known as "Tommies" and French troops were known as "poilu," which translates to "the hairy one."

Credit: Library of Congress, Prints & Photographs Division, American National Red Cross Collection

FROM DECLARATION OF WAR TO DEPLOYMENT

Although Congress declared war in early April 1917, it would be months before U.S. troops were ready for the front. The task of building a fighting force out of America's small army was given to General John J. Pershing (1860–1948). After touring the battlegrounds in France, Pershing cabled Washington, DC, to request a minimum of 1 million soldiers for the American Expeditionary Force (AEF). To win, he added, up to 3 million men might be needed.

Fielding an army of this scale required a draft, which hadn't been instituted in the United States since the Civil War. It was authorized under the Selective Service Act of May 1917. Just a few weeks later, on June 5, nearly 10 million Americans reported to register. By September, young men were reporting to boot camp by the thousands for days of 14-hour drills.

BATTLE LINES

The National Woman's Party (NWP) protested the war even after the United States joined the effort, arguing that America was fighting for democracy abroad while denying it to half of its citizens at home. Remember, American women did not have the right to vote until 1920. Countless women, including leader Alice Paul (1885–1977), were beaten and jailed for their continued suffrage activism.

For the 18 percent of foreign-born recruits, training camp also included English-language instruction and civics and citizenship instruction.

A whole host of challenges greeted military organizers, as the fresh troops needed more than basic training. Soldiers needed uniforms and munitions by the millions. Transit to Europe needed to be organized. Food supplies and medical equipment had to be secured for the field. It took months of preparations and home front support.

The decision to declare war on Germany was not unanimous. In the U.S. House of Representatives, 375 politicians voted to join the conflict and 50 voted against. In the U.S. Senate, the tally was 82 for and six against.

● ● ● ● ● ● ● ●

In 1914, Jim Crow laws in the United States allowed for legal segregation. Black reservists and enlistees in the U.S. Army fought in racially assigned regiments. New York's 369th Regiment, better-known as the Harlem Hellfighters, earned global recognition for its valor.

The 369th was among the first troops to arrive in France and saw the frontline in the spring of 1918. Their courageous actions made headlines and several members earned high French military honors. With more than 191 days in action, the Hellfighters hold the title of longest U.S. troop combat service in World War I.

Learn more in this video.

PBS righting wrong

ON THE HOME FRONT

Less than a week after the war declaration, the government launched a massive campaign to shape public opinion and educate Americans on how they could participate in the war effort. The Committee on Public Information (CPI) took inspiration from similar propaganda agencies in Great Britain, with the aim of building popular support for war.

Under the leadership of George Creel (1876–1953), CPI's 300 artists produced colorful posters, pamphlets, and advertisements that urged citizens of all races, ages, and genders to do their duty and buy war bonds and put the lid on sugar consumption. The agency also produced films, shaped news articles, and unleashed a legion of "4-Minute Men" to create favorable impressions of the war in Europe.

With the U.S. government seeking to promote its uniformly pro-war vision, laws were enacted to suppress dissenting voices. Legislation, including the Espionage Act (1917) and Sedition Act (1918), allowed government agents to censor mail and encouraged neighbors to police one another for loyalty.

The Harlem Hellfighters

Credit: National Archives

The country's 8 million German-Americans fell under particularly high degrees of scrutiny, as rumors swirled about possible German attacks on American cities. This anti-German hysteria led to changes in street names and surnames, stein-breaking fests, and the removal of German language instruction from curriculums.

Germans over the age of 14 were required to register as "aliens" and carry documentation of their status at all times. More than 6,000 of these individuals were arrested and interrogated.

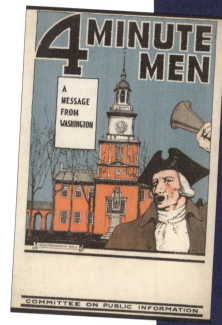

The ethnicity and immigration status of these Germans landed more than 2,000 of them in internment camps in Utah and Georgia.

The original caption of this photo reads, "German prisoners at the War Prison Camp at Fort McPherson, Georgia, engaged in the manufacture of souvenirs during their spare time. The souvenirs are sold through the prison canteen and the proceed used to buy tobacco, refreshments, etc., for the interned men. April 1918."

Credit: Mathewson and Winn

More than 75,000 4-Minute Men were recruited by the CPI to deliver rousing, 240-second speeches about the war at a range of social events and venues. These people came from all backgrounds and delivered their messages in multiple languages, from Italian to Yiddish to Sioux. Journalist George Creel (1876–1953) estimated that these orators delivered more than 7.5 million speeches to up to 400 million people during the war years.

What effect do you think this had on Americans? Take a look at this website to learn more and read some of the speeches. How do the speeches use emotion to get a reaction out of listeners?

History Matters
4-minute men

Despite being imprisoned during the 1920 campaign for president, Eugene V. Debs still earned 3.5 percent of the vote.

● ● ● ● ● ● ● ●

Politicians and activists who voiced anti-war opinions also faced intense scrutiny and potential imprisonment, as were those who objected on religious, moral, and ethical grounds. Public school teacher Mary Stone McDowell (1876–1955) was dismissed from her position at a high school in Brooklyn, New York, because, as a Quaker and pacifist, she refused to pledge a loyalty oath.

Politicians such as Senator Robert La Follette (1855–1925) of Wisconsin and Eugene V. Debs (1855–1926), leader of the Socialist Party of America, risked alienation and ostracism as they maintained their anti-war positions. Debs was even sentenced to 10 years in prison for seditious activity after he proclaimed, "The working class have never yet had a voice in declaring a war." Debs served a two-and-a-half-year sentence at a federal penitentiary in Georgia before having his sentence commuted by U.S. President Warren G. Harding (1865–1923) in 1921.

While wartime curtailed the rights of millions, it created opportunities for others. More than 1 million women entered the workplace as temporary employees of factories and offices, filling positions vacated by soldiers fighting overseas.

Women also took on newly created jobs to support the supply needs of Allied troops.

In addition, women led various home-front efforts to conserve food, knit clothing, and lead fundraising efforts. In the period after the war, the contributions and support of women continued to have influence, opening the door to conversations about civil rights in American culture and, eventually, the right to vote.

AMERICANS ON THE WESTERN FRONT

When the first 14,500 U.S. soldiers arrived in France in late June 1917, General Pershing deemed them unready and ill-prepared for the realities of combat. The American Expeditionary Force set up European training camps to further familiarize the doughboys with equipment provided by the French and British militaries. It wasn't until October that the first AEF troops engaged in combat.

U.S. forces continued to trickle into France in 1917 and early 1918. They arrived in greater numbers in time for a key turning point—with the war with Russia essentially over in the East, Germany diverted troops to mount key offensives on the Western Front. Aiming to break the stalemate, General Ludendorff planned five such attacks between March and July 1918.

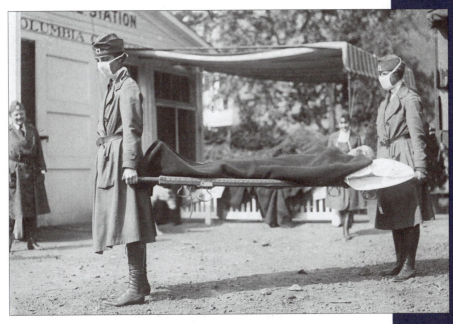

Red Cross workers demonstrate how to transport a patient via stretcher.

A GLOBAL PANDEMIC

Fall 1918 saw another threat to people around the world—influenza. This strain of the flu virus swept through barracks, bunkers, and hospitals. It crossed the Atlantic on military vessels, infecting millions across multiple continents. Just as they did during the COVID-19 pandemic beginning in 2020, public health officials tried to contain it by limiting public gatherings. By the time it waned in 1920, more than one-third of the world's population had been infected and more than 21 million people had died. As of February 2022, COVID-19 had killed more than 5 million people globally. In the United States, more people died from COVID-19 than from influenza a century earlier.

Native Americans played a critical role in both combat and communications on the Western Front. Choctaw soldiers used their language—undecipherable by German code breakers—to transmit critical pieces of intelligence. The U.S. military capitalized on unique, Indigenous languages again in World War II, deploying Navajo Code Talkers.

Watch this video to learn more about this communications team.

Ann Wolf Navajo code

But each offensive proved weaker than the one before. Then, Ludendorff spiraled toward a nervous breakdown after the death of his stepson on the battlefields of France. German soldiers were dying and deserting in massive numbers. The chances of a Central Power victory were disappearing with them.

As Germany's troops depleted, the Allies found reinforcement in their American associates. In the war's final six months, newly arrived U.S. troops tipped the balance of personnel, helping to halt the German advance and turn the tide toward an Allied victory.

Despite the good news, from September 26 until the armistice on November 11, many of these men saw fierce fighting in the deadliest battle in U.S. history, the seven-week Meuse-Argonne Offensive.

TEXT TO WORLD

What stereotypes do you live with or witness in your life?

KEY QUESTIONS

- How did different opinions about the war reflect the diversity of America's population?

- How did Americans of a variety of backgrounds participate in the war effort?

- What impact did American participation in the war have on its outcome?

AMERICANS CHANGE THEIR TUNE ON WAR

In the early part of the twentieth century, popular songs served as an avenue for sharing news, promoting viewpoints, and making sense of current events. Music from this era provides a unique window into shifting public opinion on America's role in the war.

- **Go to the library or use the internet to investigate the history of Tin Pan Alley, a group of songwriters and music publishers who dominated the landscape of popular music in America in the nineteenth and twentieth centuries.**

  - What influence did music exert on public opinion during this era?

  - How were songs used to shape patriotism and public opinion?

- **In the spring of 1915, America's hit song was "I Didn't Raise My Boy to Be a Soldier."** In 1917, audiences across the country were singing a different tune, "Over There." Compare the lyrics of the two songs (found on the following pages) and answer the following questions.

  - Who are the audiences?

  - What appeal is being made to them?

  - How does each song play on the listener's emotions?

  - What does the shift in popular music lyrics indicate about possible large-scale shifts in public opinion?

VOCAB LAB 📖

Write down what you think each word means. What root words can you find to help you? What does the context of the word tell you?

censor, internment camp, isolationist, Jim Crow, ostracism, recession, seditious, and **temperance**

Compare your definitions with those of your friends or classmates. Did you all come up with the same meanings? Turn to the text and glossary if you need help.

VICTORY GARDENS

During the war, Americans on the home front were encouraged to do their part by conserving food. First Lady Edith Wilson (1872–1961) pledged to abstain from wheat, meat, and sugar. Millions of others followed her lead. Edith and Woodrow Wilson also transformed the White House lawn into a pasture for sheep—the wool was sold to raise money for American troops. Across the country, Victory Gardens cropped up. Civilians were encouraged to tend small plots and grow their own food to allow for larger harvests to be sent to Europe.

I Didn't Raise My Boy to Be a Soldier (1915)

Ten million soldiers to the war have gone,
Who may never return again.
Ten million mothers' hearts must break,
For the ones who died in vain.
Head bowed down in sorrow in her lonely years,
I heard a mother murmur thro' her tears:

  Chorus:

I didn't raise my boy to be a soldier,
I brought him up to be my pride and joy,
Who dares to put a musket on his shoulder,
To shoot some other mother's darling boy?
Let nations arbitrate their future troubles,
It's time to lay the sword and gun away,
There'd be no war today,
If mothers all would say,
I didn't raise my boy to be a soldier.

What victory can cheer a mother's heart,
When she looks at her blighted home?
What victory can bring her back,
All she cared to call her own?
Let each mother answer in the year to be,
Remember that my boy belongs to me!

Source: Al Piantadosi and Alfred Bryan, "I Didn't Raise My Boy To Be a Soldier."

Over There (1917)

Johnnie, get your gun, get your
    gun, get your gun,
Take it on the run, on the run, on the run,
Hear them calling you and me,
Ev'ry son of liberty.
Hurry right away, no delay, go today,
Make your daddy glad to have had such a lad,
Tell your sweetheart not to pine,
To be proud her boy's in line.

    Chorus:

Over there over there
Send the word, send the word over there
That the Yanks are coming, the Yanks are coming,
The drums rum-tumming ev'rywhere
So prepare say a pray'r
Send the word, send the word to beware
We'll be over, we're coming over,
And we won't come back till it's over over there!

Johnnie, get your gun, get your
    gun, get your gun,
Johnnie, show the Hun you're a son of a gun,
Hoist the flag and let her fly,
Yankee Doodle do or die.
Pack your little kit, show your grit, do your bit,
Yankees to the ranks from the
    towns and the tanks,
Make your mother proud of you
And the old Red White and Blue.

Source: George M. Cohan, Composer

**Inquire &
Investigate**

To investigate more, consider that in conflicts later in the twentieth century, musicians continued to use their medium to comment on war. Research the role that music played in expressing opposition to and support for conflicts ranging from World War II to the Vietnam War to the First Gulf War. How was this music similar to that of WWI? How was it different?

OLD WOUNDS CONTINUE TO BE REOPENED DESPITE PEACE THAT HAD BEEN BROKERED.

How does World War I continue to influence the world today?

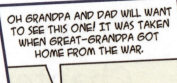

On the "eleventh hour of the eleventh day of the eleventh month," World War I came to a halt. The agreed-upon ceasefire meant the guns went quiet, the planes landed, and soldiers stopped shooting across No Man's Land. It was a time of celebration—and relief. But the policies that grew from the agreements made after the war led to further carnage in World War II and still cause repercussions around the world in the twenty-first century.

The moment of ceasefire, when men on both sides erupted from their trenches and mingled together without fear of death or retribution, carried echoes of the Christmas truce that swept the Western Front almost four years earlier. But would this peace and spontaneous display of goodwill hold in the years and decades to come?

In a world of uncertainty and change, that remained to be seen. The possibility of a lasting peace would be decided by the terms of the armistice, treaties, and yet-to-be-established social, economic, and political developments. No one could know the future.

LAY DOWN YOUR ARMS

By August 1918, the German war effort was in crisis. On the home front, skyrocketing food prices led to massive social unrest. On the Western Front, disillusioned soldiers deserted in droves.

The German high command knew that peace talks were inevitable, especially with their combat partners Bulgaria and Austria-Hungary asking the Allies to come to the negotiating table. But General Ludendorff wanted conditions for the talks to be as favorable as possible and prolonged the war effort. Ludendorff also thought that President Wilson, with his vision of "peace without victory," would establish fairer terms than Great Britain and France. With Wilson's "Fourteen Points" in mind, the Germans appealed directly to the United States.

Five weeks lapsed between the armistice request in early October and its signing on November 11, during which telegraphs filled with negotiations volleyed across the Atlantic. But the German hopes that the Americans would offer more lenient terms were soon dashed.

Germany wanted to retain the lands it conquered in 1914, but Wilson rejected that proposition. Wilson also suggested that peace would require the abdication of Kaiser Wilhelm II and the establishment of a representative democracy.

The revolution in Berlin caused the Kaiser to step down and flee Germany.

Credit: National Library of Scotland (CC BY 4.0)

"**I was the only audience for the greatest show ever presented.** On both sides of no-man's-land, the trenches erupted. Brown-uniformed men poured out of the American trenches, gray-green uniforms out of the German. . . . Seconds before they had been willing to shoot each other; now they came forward. Hesitantly at first, then more quickly, each group approached the other.

Suddenly gray uniforms mixed with brown. I could see them hugging each other, dancing, jumping. . . . I flew up to the French sector. There it was even more incredible. After four years of slaughter and hatred, they were not only hugging each other but kissing each other on both cheeks as well.

Star shells, rockets and flares began to go up, and I turned my ship toward the field. The war was over."

—American aviator Eddie Rickenbacker (1890–1973) on his bird's-eye view of WWI's armistice taking effect

Watch footage of the revolution in Berlin. What seems to be the general mood in the city?

Pathe Revolution in Berlin

BATTLE LINES

The railcar in which the armistice agreement was signed was captured by the Nazis during World War II. In 1940, Hitler forced France to sign an armistice agreement in the very same carriage at the very same site in the Forest of Compiègne. It was then brought back to Berlin as a trophy of victory.

The kaiser's abdication was sped up by mutinying sailors in the port of Kiel on November 3 who also demanded he resign. The rebellion quickly spread to Hamburg, Bremen, and Munich. By November 9, the citizens of Berlin took to the streets in the spirit of revolution, demanding a kaiser-less and democratic Germany. That day, the kaiser stepped down and fled the country for neighboring Netherlands.

At the same time Berliners were rebelling, diplomats from both sides were meeting in secret in the railcar of Supreme Allied Commander Ferdinand Foch (1851–1929), deep in the Forest of Compiègne. The armistice agreement presented by the Allies required a ceasefire plus:

- Germany must surrender occupied territories in France and Belgium.

- Germany must surrender all war materiel, including warships and airplanes.

- The Allies would occupy German territory west of the Rhine River.

- The naval blockade would persist until a peace treaty was signed.

It was agreed that war would officially cease at 11 a.m. In those final six hours of the bloodiest conflict the world had yet seen, 11,000 more soldiers were killed, wounded, or went missing.

CRAFTING THE PEACE

The armistice signaled a ceasefire, not a lasting and permanent peace. That task fell to the Paris Peace Conference, which convened in January 1919. Representatives from 27 countries participated in the process, but neither Germany nor Russia were invited to shape the development of the treaty.

The peacemakers had a massive task. In the previous four years, the world had been fundamentally reshaped. Monarchies and empires had crumbled. People under colonial rule had demanded to govern themselves. A Soviet state had been born in Russia. Amid this turbulent climate, the world's diplomats sought to establish some semblance of order. Plus, they had to reconcile their own conflicting goals, all with an eye toward the public opinion of the populations they represented.

Each year on November 11, Armistice Day is commemorated in many Allied countries. The poppy, first used as a symbol of veterans' sacrifice in 1919, is often incorporated into public remembrances. Today, veterans' support groups in the United States and elsewhere sell poppy seed packets and boutonnieres to fundraise for veterans with disabilities.

The delegates in Paris had two tasks: establish punishment and build a better world. Do you think these two jobs were complementary or contradictory?

First, the delegates assigned guilt and blame for the war. This landed squarely on the shoulders of Germany. At the same time, they worked to build a new world order out of the ashes of the old. This movement was led by Woodrow Wilson, who proposed a League of Nations that would reach some kind of agreement among the countries. It would also lead worldwide efforts toward disarmament, cooperation, and peace.

BATTLE LINES

Much to the disappointment of President Wilson, the U.S. Congress did not ratify the Treaty of Versailles. This meant that the United States, a rising political and economic superpower, did not join the League of Nations. Instead, as promised by Wilson's successor, Warren G. Harding, the country reverted to a policy of isolationism.

After six months of heated negotiations—Japanese and Italian delegates both bowed out over disputes about borders and promised territorial gains—the Treaty of Versailles was signed on June 28, 1919, five years to the date after the assassination of Franz Ferdinand. Its 440 articles spelled out the formation of the League of Nations. It also extended harsh and punitive terms on Germany's government. In addition to loss of territories and military equipment, the treaty demanded a major contraction of the nation's armed forces.

Most notably, Germany was tasked with paying for all war damages. This meant the country was at great risk for bankruptcy and hyperinflation, which in turn paved the way for widespread resentment.

It was a fatal flaw recognized by the conference organizers, including French General Ferdinand Foch, who famously remarked that it wasn't so much a peace treaty as a "20-year armistice." As it turned out, this wouldn't be the "war to end all wars." Its untidy and harsh conclusion would set the stage for a century of global conflict.

The U.S. 64th Regiment celebrates the armistice
Credit: U.S. National Archive

THE WAR'S AFTERMATH

From Palestine to Petrograd, from Berlin and Belgrade, aftershocks from the war persisted long after the Treaty of Versailles. Across Europe, cities and towns were missing their young, male populations.

Germany lost 35 percent of its men between the ages of 19 and 22. France lost half of its male population who were ages 20 to 32 at the outbreak of war.

Millions of wounded and traumatized troops returned to points across the globe. Each and every one of these soldiers belonged to communities that either mourned their absence or sought to reintegrate them after the war.

On a larger scale, the effects of the war and the fragile peace that followed also rippled into the decades to come. The genocidal policies of the Nazis during World War II, the continued violence over land in the Balkans, and ethnic and religious tensions in the Middle East all trace their roots to the events of 1914 through 1918.

BATTLE LINES

A 1937 Gallup poll showed that 70 percent of Americans believed that U.S. involvement in World War I was "a mistake."

Only 22 years after the end of World War I, World War II erupted, involving many of the same countries. This is a scene from the invasion of Normandy Beach in France in 1944.

Throughout the 1920s, a chorus of voices in Germany blamed the country's war loss on dissidents and "internal enemies" who, they claimed, "stabbed Germany in the back."

Rather than placing responsibility on military leaders and politicians, extremists made scapegoats out of leftists, liberals, and the country's Jewish population.

The figure who articulated these conspiracy theories most vocally and murderously was war veteran Adolf Hitler. The roots of the Holocaust—which claimed more than 11 million lives—lie partially in the campaign of hate that followed the First World War and simmered for more than a decade.

Four empires—the Ottoman, Austro-Hungarian, Russian, and German—collapsed as a direct result of the war. Out of their demise, the new nations of Austria, Czechoslovakia, Estonia, Hungary, Latvia, Lithuania, and Turkey rose.

So, too, did Communist Russia. The shift of power in Russia from a monarchy to Bolshevik rule unleashed a wave of what were known as Red Scares, or panic about communism. From France to Germany to the United States, fear and paranoia about the spread of the Communist Revolution led to suppression of political speech and action.

World War I erupted in the Balkan Peninsula over questions about who had the right to govern which lands and peoples. The war did not resolve these conflicts. Through the 1990s and into the 2000s, violent wars of independence and insurgencies raged in the region, with genocidal consequences in Bosnia and Herzegovina.

BATTLE LINES

After the war, the British seized control of the areas that are today Iraq, Israel, and Jordan. France took control of Lebanon and Syria. In 1917, the British pledged support for the creation of a "national home for the Jewish people" in the region.

Arab groups that joined the Allies in the Middle East to fight against the Ottoman Empire had been promised a new future by the British and French. The future delivered, however, was far from what Arab leaders had envisioned. Britain and France partitioned the region into new states, drawing borders with little consideration for the histories of those who lived within them. Each power occupied areas based on strategic transportation and resource interests. Instead of self-rule, these new countries gained decades of European occupation.

WAVES OF CHANGE

Let's look at three ways World War I altered the economic and social character of the world.

New Economic Powers: The war shifted the world's center of economic power from London to New York. Because of American financial lending and wartime production, the U.S. dollar became the new global currency.

New Political Opportunities: In the United States, the participation of disenfranchised groups in the war had mixed results. Women received the right to vote shortly after the war and saw new opportunities in the decade that followed.

In many places, returning African American soldiers weren't greeted with respect and gratitude for their service. Instead, they experienced an onslaught of violence from whites who feared they'd claim new rights and seek new employment opportunities. The summer of 1919 saw racially motivated mob violence in cities from Washington, DC, to Chicago, Illinois. Hundreds of African Americans and supporters died as a result of this violence. Out of the experience, African American communities formed new efforts to obtain civil rights.

LEAGUE OF NATIONS 2.0: THE UNITED NATIONS

As World War II loomed over Europe in the late 1930s, it became clear that the League of Nations had failed to fulfill its central aim of maintaining peace. A new organization was envisioned to promote international peace and prevent war—the United Nations (UN). The new organization's charter was ratified on October 24, 1945. During its decades-long existence, three essential pillars have structured UN activities: peace and security, human rights, and development. Today, there are 193 member states. One of the best-known documents produced by the UN, the Universal Declaration of Human Rights (UDHR), was drafted in 1948. The UDHR continues to guide global citizens in recognizing their inalienable rights, which all other residents of the planet are entitled to. Why is this important?

WAR IN UKRAINE

In February 2022, Vladimir Putin ordered forces to invade the country of Ukraine under the pretense of protecting Russians. Millions of civilians fled to neighboring countries while others stayed to fight. Governments around the world condemned Putin's actions and applied economic sanctions, even as crowds within Russia protested the war. People wondered: Could this develop into World War III? We hope the lessons learned during wars of the past will carry into the future, but democracy takes work and memory. As of this printing, the fate of Ukraine is still unknown.

● ● ● ● ● ● ●

TEXT TO WORLD

How might your life be different if WWI had never been fought?

Changing Forms of Expression: The war's seemingly senseless violence also influenced art and literature. Poets, painters, and musicians explored the randomness of the war in their works. From Dadaism—which rejected the conventions of modern society and embraced irrationalism—to the avant-garde poetry of E.E. Cummings, the war prompted a rupture with traditional forms of expression.

A CENTURY LATER

On November 11, 2018, the world's leaders gathered in Paris to commemorate the 100th anniversary of the armistice that ended World War I. There, at the foot of the Arc de Triomphe, French President Emmanuel Macron (1977–) delivered a message of remembrance mixed with notes of warning. "The traces of this war never went away," he told those assembled. He continued to caution against the "old demons" of nationalism, which in Europe and elsewhere are "rising again."

How will we—as individuals and citizens of the world—grapple with and fight against these demons? How can we use the lessons of the past as we face the future?

And will we, as a world community, rise to the challenge that Macron proposed on that rainy November day in 2018 "to wage the only battle worth waging: the battle for peace, the battle for a better world."

World leaders marked the 100th anniversary of World War I's armistice in Paris on November 11, 2018.

Credit: The Kremlin, Moscow (CC BY 4.0 International)

From the Eastern Front to the Western Front and from Anatolia to Australia to Algeria, the First World War was one of a truly global scale. Behind every battle on land, sea, and air, there were individual lives on every continent threaded together by bloodshed, devastation, and loss. Whether an Irish nationalist, French schoolboy, American pacifist or war hawk, the war reshaped the lives and perspectives of all the world's inhabitants.

It's this world that we have inherited. We owe it to those who lived through its trauma to remember the pain and suffering that defined those years.

KEY QUESTIONS

- **What were some of the key flaws of the Treaty of Versailles?**

- **How did World War I pave the way for later conflicts, including World War II?**

- **Where and how do we see the continued impact of World War I?**

Inquire & Investigate

VOCAB LAB 📖

Write down what you think each word means. What root words can you find to help you? What does the context of the word tell you?

avant-garde, **Dadaism**, **disarmament**, **dissident**, **hyperinflation**, **nationalism**, and **reparations**

Compare your definitions with those of your friends or classmates. Did you all come up with the same meanings? Turn to the text and glossary if you need help.

THE BONUS ARMY

On their return from fighting in Europe, U.S. veterans of the war were promised a cash bonus. But they'd have to wait until 1945—27 years—to collect it. The dire economic circumstances of the Great Depression led many who served to take direct action, marching on and camping out in Washington, DC, to demand a more immediate payout.

• **Read or listen to this NPR piece on the history of the Bonus Army.** Then, answer the following.

  • When, where, and why did the Bonus Army form?

  • Who made up the Bonus Army?

  • What were the Bonus Army's goals and demands?

  • How did the Bonus Army go about pursuing its aims?

• **Reread the article.** Do you think that the Bonus Army was successful in achieving its aims? Why or why not? Write a paragraph stating your claim, supported by evidence and reasoning.

> To investigate more, consider that the article concludes by noting that the Bonus Army's actions paved the way for the G.I. Bill. Research this legislation. When and why it was passed? What resources and services did it offer American veterans?

NPR Bonus Army

REMEMBERING 100 YEARS ON

The year 2018 marked 100 years since the end of World War I. Around the globe, memorials were designed to reflect on the lasting impact of the conflict. After the war, monuments and memorials sprung up in cities and towns across Europe to honor those who lost their lives. In London, the Cenotaph was unveiled in 1919.

- **Research the history of this memorial.**

  - Who commissioned it, and who designed it? Why was it seen as important to have a war memorial of this scale in London?

  - What was the popular reception at the time?

  - How did people interact with the Cenotaph? How has that changed with time?

- **Investigate temporary installations designed to mark the 100th anniversary of the war's end.** Here are some pieces of art you might consider. How do these twenty-first century efforts to remember differ in form from earlier memorials?

Artist Rob Heard's *Shrouds of the Somme*, London

Paul Cummins/Tom Piper's *Weeping Window*, London

Never Again poppy installation, Munich

To investigate more, consider how military dress continued to change through the twentieth century and into the twenty-first. Look at various wars and conflicts to see how the clothing of soldiers was modified for fighting conditions and new technologies.

GLOSSARY

abdicate: to give up or renounce one's position of power.

abstain: to keep from doing.

activist: a person who works for social or political change.

adaptation: the act of adjusting.

advocate: to publicly support something.

agricultural: describes growing crops and raising animals for food.

alienate: to cause someone to feel isolated.

alliance: a partnership between peoples or countries.

Allied Powers: the countries that fought together against Germany and the Central Powers during World War I, including Great Britain, France, Russia, and the United States.

alms: something given freely to help the poor.

amplify: to make a sound louder or an issue more well known.

anarchist: a person who does not believe that government and laws are necessary and wants to abolish them.

anarchy: a society without a strong government.

Anatolia: a peninsula in southwestern Asia that forms the Asian part of Turkey.

annexation: the addition of a new territory or area to an original area.

anti-Semitism: prejudice or hostility toward Jewish people.

Arabian Peninsula: a peninsula between the Red Sea and the Persian Gulf that is strategically important for its oil resources.

arbitration: the process where someone settles a dispute between other people.

armistice: an agreement or truce between opposing sides in a war to stop fighting.

artillery: a division of the army that handles large weapons. Also large guns used to shoot over a great distance.

assassinate: to murder an important person for political or religious reasons.

atrocity: a cruel act of violence.

attrition: to try to win by wearing down an enemy, with knowledge that continued combat will result in major losses for both sides.

autocrat: someone who has complete power in a country or organization.

avant-garde: an experimental style of art.

Baltic States: European countries bordering the Baltic Sea.

bankruptcy: a legal proceeding involving a person or business that is unable to repay outstanding debts.

Bedouin: a member of a nomadic tribe of Arabs.

besiege: to attack vigorously.

blockade: the sealing off of a place to prevent people and goods from entering or leaving.

Bolshevik: a member of the left-wing majority group of the Russian Social Democratic Workers' Party, later known as a Communist. The Russian socialist party favored a revolution to seize power in Russia for the purpose of setting up a workers' state.

bombardment: a constant attack.

byproduct: an extra and sometimes unexpected or unintended result of an action or process.

caravan: a large group of people traveling together.

casualty: a person who is injured or killed during war.

Caucasus: the mountain range in Caucasia between the Black Sea and the Caspian Sea that forms part of the traditional border between Europe and Asia.

cede: to surrender something to another.

censor: when the government examines material for the public, such as books, newspapers, or the news, and removes information it does not approve of.

Central Powers: the group of countries that fought against the Allies in WWI, including Germany, Austria-Hungary, Bulgaria, and the Ottoman Empire.

chronic: recurring.

citizen: a person who has all the rights and responsibilities that come with being a full member of a country.

civilian: a member of society who is not in the military.

civilization: a society having a relatively high level of cultural and technological development.

civilized: describes a community of people with a highly developed culture and social organization.

coalition: a combination or alliance, especially a temporary one between persons, groups, or states.

colonize: to take control of an area and the people who live there.

colonizer: the person, group, or country that takes control of a region and the people there.

colony: a country or area that is under the political control of another country.

commandeer: to take possession of something.

commemorate: to remember and honor.

communism: an economic and political system in which the government owns everything used in the production and distribution of goods.

commute: to reduce a judicial sentence to one less severe.

complement: to complete or enhance by providing something additional.

concentration camp: a place where large numbers of people, especially political prisoners or persecuted minorities, are imprisoned.

conscription: the drafting of men into military service.

conspiracy theory: the belief that a circumstance or event is caused and controlled by secret forces.

conspirator: a person involved in a secret plan to do harm.

context: the background or setting.

contradict: to state the opposite of someone else's statement.

convoy: a group of ships or vehicles traveling together, typically protected by armed troops, warships, or other vehicles.

crops: plants grown for food and other uses.

cultural: relating to a culture or civilization or to the arts.

cultural identity: the behavior, interests, desires, and passions of a group of people.

culture: the beliefs and way of life of a group of people, which can include religion, language, art, clothing, food, and holidays.

Dadaism: an art movement that went against traditional ideas of beauty and cultural value.

decadent: a state of moral or cultural decline or something that is richly extravagant.

dehumanize: to treat someone or make someone feel as if they aren't human.

deport: to expel a foreigner from a country.

diplomat: a person who represents one country to another.

diplomatic: concerned with communication between countries.

disarmament: to reduce or withdraw military forces and weapons.

disenfranchised: deprived of a right or privilege, especially the right to vote.

disillusioned: feeling disappointment from finding out that something isn't as good as it was thought to be.

dispatch: a message.

dissent: disagreement with a widely held opinion.

dissident: a person who disagrees with a widely held opinion.

diverse: many different people or things.

diversity: variety; when referring to people, diversity means including individuals of varied race, gender, or cultures.

divine: related to a god.

dove: a person who opposes war.

draft: a government requirement that men join the military.

dreadnought: a state-of-the-art battleship built in the early twentieth century

Eastern Front: during World War I, the fighting that took place in the east between the Russian Empire on one side and the Central Powers on the other.

economic: having to do with the resources and wealth of a country.

electroshock therapy: the treatment of mental illness and especially depression by the application of electric current to the head.

elite: people with the most wealth or the highest status.

empire: a group of countries, states, or lands that are ruled by one person or family.

enlist: to enroll in the military.

ethnic: a group of people of the same race or nationality who share a distinctive culture.

ethnicity: the cultural identity of a person, including language, religion, nationality, customs, and ancestry.

experiential: learning from direct observation or activity.

famine: a period of great hunger and lack of food for a large population of people.

fervor: great feeling.

fiber: a long, thin thread that makes up cloth materials such as cotton or linen.

figurative: using words in a non-literal way.

fortified: strengthened with walls and trenches.

Fourteen Points: Woodrow Wilson's proposal of conditions that would create a lasting peace after World War I.

front: the dividing point where two armies meet.

gender: male or female, and their roles or behavior defined by society.

GLOSSARY

genocide: the deliberate killing of a large group of people based on race, ethnicity, or nationality.

global: relating to the entire world.

globalization: the integration of the world economy through trade, money, and labor.

guru: a teacher or an expert.

hallucination: seeing, hearing, or smelling something that seems real but does not exist.

hawk: a person who takes a pro-war position.

Holocaust: a time before and during World War II when the German Nazis tried to kill the entire Jewish race, as well as several other groups.

hostage: a person held against their will by another person or group in order to ensure demands are met.

hostel: an overnight facility.

hostility: anger or violence directed at another.

human rights: the rights that belong to all people, such as freedom from torture, the right to live, and freedom from slavery.

humanize: to give something a human character.

hyperinflation: extreme economic inflation with prices rising at a very high rate in a very short time.

hysteria: exaggerated or uncontrollable emotion or excitement.

immigrant: a person who leaves his or her own country to live in another country.

indigenous: describes a person who is a native to a place.

Industrial Revolution: a period during the eighteenth and nineteenth centuries when large cities and factories began to replace small towns and farming.

industry: the large-scale production of goods, especially in factories.

inequality: differences in opportunity and treatment based on social, ethnic, racial, or economic qualities.

inferior: lower in rank or status or quality.

infrastructure: basic facilities such as roads, power plants, and communication systems.

injustice: something that is very unfair or unequal.

insurgency: a revolt, uprising.

internment camp: a place where people are confined or imprisoned.

interrogate: to ask someone, such as a prisoner or criminal, a lot of questions in an angry or threatening way in order to get information.

irrationalism: the belief system that counters or contradicts rational ideas.

isolationist: someone who follows a policy of remaining apart from and uninvolved with the politics of other countries.

Jim Crow: the practice of discriminating against and segregating African Americans through legal enforcement and social sanctions in the South in the United States, beginning in the late eighteenth century.

justice: fair treatment under the law.

League of Nations: An intergovernmental organization formed after World War I to promote and maintain world peace

lenient: a light punishment.

liberty: the freedom to live as you wish or go where you want.

looting: taking something by dishonesty, force, or stealth.

mandatory: required.

marginalization: treatment of a person as unimportant or powerless within a society or group.

materiel: military materials and equipment.

meme: a cultural item in the form of an image, video, or phrase that is spread by the internet and altered in a humorous way.

metaphor: a figure of speech in which a word is used to symbolize another word.

mobilize: to prepare a military.

momentum: the tendency of a moving object to keep moving.

morale: the confidence and enthusiasm of a person or group.

munitions: materials used in war, especially weapons and ammunition.

mutiny: a revolt or rebellion against authority.

nation state: a state containing one, as opposed to several, nationalities.

nationalism: devotion or loyalty to one's country, patriotism.

nationalist: someone who believes that one's own country is superior to others and places primary emphasis on the promotion of its culture and interests.

nationality: the status of belonging to a particular nation.

neutral: not favoring one side over another.

neutrality: the policy of a country not to participate in wars between other countries.

occupation: in war, the act of invading and then controlling another country.

offensive: an attacking military campaign.

onslaught: a fierce attack.

ordain: to order by virtue of superior authority.

ore: a naturally occurring mineral that contains metal.

ostracism: being excluded from a group.

Ottoman Empire: an empire based in Turkey that controlled North Africa, southern Europe, and Southwest Asia.

pacifist: a person who is opposed to war or violence.

panorama: a wide, unobstructed view in all directions.

paramilitary: a military group or organization that is not part of a country's armed forces.

partition: to divide up into smaller parts.

patriotism: devotion to and love for one's country.

persecute: to abuse or ill-treat someone based on their race or political or religious beliefs.

persecution: a campaign to exterminate or drive away a group of people based on their religious beliefs or other characteristic.

personification: to imagine that an object has human or animal characteristics or that an animal has human characteristics.

petition: a written request signed by many people.

pioneer: one of the first to use or apply a new area of knowledge or one of the first to settle in a new land.

pogrom: an organized massacre of a particular group.

political: relating to running a government and holding onto power.

principality: a state ruled by a prince.

profit: financial gain; income less expenses.

proletariat: a term that philosopher Karl Marx used to describe the working classes.

propaganda: biased, misleading, or false information that is promoted to persuade people to believe a certain viewpoint.

proverb: a short pithy saying stating a general truth or piece of advice.

province: a district or region of some countries.

provisional: temporary, existing for the time being.

provisions: food, drink, or equipment for a long journey.

punitive: action taken to punish a state or group of persons.

radical: a person with extreme political or social views.

ratify: to officially approve something.

raw material: a natural resource used to make something.

rebel: to fight against authority or a person who fights against authority.

rebellion: defying authority or an organized attempt to overthrow a government or other authority.

recession: a temporary economic slowdown.

reconnaissance: the military observation or investigation of an enemy.

recruit: to enlist new people to a cause or army or someone who recently joined the armed forces or another group.

reforms: changes to improve something.

refugee: a person forced to flee because of war, persecution, or a natural disaster.

reintegrate: to unite or bring a separate unit back into a whole.

reparations: compensation for war damage that is paid by the losing power.

respirator: a device that helps with breathing.

restraint: the act of holding back and keeping under control.

retaliate: to fight back.

retreat: to move away from the enemy in battle.

retribution: a punishment inflicted on someone as vengeance.

revered: to respect and worship.

revolution: a dramatic, widespread change in society.

riot: a gathering of people protesting something that gets out of control and violent.

sabotage: the planned destruction of property or an act that interferes with work or another activity.

satire: humor used to exaggerate and reveal people's stupidity or political foolishness.

scapegoat: a person or group that bears the blame for others.

scroll: a piece of paper or parchment with writing on it that is rolled into the shape of a tube.

seditious: describing conduct or speech that promotes rebellion against a government.

GLOSSARY

segregation: the enforced separation of different racial groups in a community or country.

shellshock: a psychological condition resulting from the trauma of combat.

shrapnel: fragment of an explosive object.

sickle: a sharp farming tool in the shape of a half moon.

simile: a figure of speech that compares two different things using the words like or as.

simulate: to imitate certain conditions for the purpose of testing or study.

sniper: a skilled shooter who shoots at other people from a concealed place.

social: living in groups.

socialist: combining capitalist and communist methods. The government provides services but private property is allowed.

sovereignty: government free from external control.

sparring: fighting.

stalemate: a contest where neither side is winning.

statistics: numbers that show facts about a subject.

status: the position or rank of one group in society compared to another group.

steppe: a large, flat grassland with no trees that stretches across a cool, dry region of Europe and Asia.

stereotype: a judgment about a group of individuals or the inaccurate belief that all people who share a single physical or cultural trait are the same.

strike: an organized protest in which people refuse to work until changes are made in the workplace.

subversive: someone trying to destroy or damage something, especially a political system.

suffrage: the right to vote in political elections.

surge: to move forward as a large mass very quickly.

superiority: having an advantage over or being more powerful than someone or something.

suppress: to prevent an event from happening.

technology: the tools, methods, and systems used to solve a problem or do work.

temperance: the practice of drinking little or no alcohol.

terrorist: a person who uses violence and threats to frighten people.

textiles: having to do with cloth and weaving.

toll: the number of deaths, casualties, or injuries arising from particular circumstances, such as a battle or war.

Treaty of Versailles: a peace treaty signed in 1919 that ended World War I. It forced Germany to take responsibility for the war and to pay reparations.

treaty: a formal agreement among countries.

trench warfare: when opposing troops fight from ditches facing each other.

Triple Entente: an informal agreement between France, Russia, and Great Britain prior to the First World War that established their alliance.

troops: a group of soldiers.

tsar: a Russian king.

tuberculosis: a deadly disease of the lungs.

tyrant: a cruel ruler who denies people their rights.

U-boats: German submarines.

ultimatum: a final demand.

unanimous: when a decision or action is agreed upon by everyone involved.

uncouth: without manners.

unification: the process of uniting or bringing together.

Union Jack: the national flag of the United Kingdom.

unprecedented: never done or known before.

valor: the quality of being very brave, especially in war.

vantage point: a place or position affording a good view of something.

veteran: someone who has served in the military.

vitality: the state of being strong, active, energetic.

war bond: an investment issued by a government to finance military operations during times of war.

weapons of mass destruction: weapons capable of causing widespread death and destruction.

Western Front: In World War I, the fighting that took place in Belgium and France between the Allied Powers and Germany.

World War I (1914–1918): also known as the Great War, fought between the Allied Powers (Russia, France, Great Britain, United States, and others) and the Central Powers (Germany, Austro-Hungarian Empire, Ottoman Empire, and others) and won by the Allies.

zeppelin: a large German dirigible or airship, similar to a blimp.

RESESOURCES

RESOURCES

BOOKS

Fleming, Candace. *The Family Romanov: Murder, Rebellion, & the Fall of Imperial Russia*. Random House Children's Books, 2014.

Grant, R.G., and Richard Overy. *World War I: The Definitive Visual Guide: From Sarajevo to Versailles*. Dorling Kindersley, 2018.

Hale, Nathan. *Treaties, Trenches, Mud, and Blood: A World War I Tale*. Scholastic, 2017.

Marrin, Albert. *Very, Very Dreadful: The Influenza Pandemic of 1918*. Random House, 2018.

Morpurgo, Michael, et al. *The Great War: Stories Inspired by Items from the First World War*. Candlewick Press, 2019.

Murphy, Jim. *Truce: The Day the Soldiers Stopped Fighting*. Scholastic Press, 2009.

Myers, Walter Dean. *The Harlem Hellfighters: When Pride Met Courage*. HarperCollins, 2006.

WEBSITES

"America at War: World War I." *Digital History*, University of Houston, 2016. digitalhistory.uh.edu/era.cfm?eraID=12&smtID=2

Beauchamp, Zack, et al. "40 Maps That Explain World War I." *Vox.com*, 4 Aug. 2014. vox.com/a/world-war-i-maps

"Echoes of the Great War: American Experiences of World War I." The Library of Congress loc.gov/exhibitions/world-war-i-american-experiences/about-this-exhibition

"First World War and the End of the Habsburg Monarchy." *Der Erste Weltkrieg*, Schloß Schönbrunn Kultur- Und Betriebsges.m.b.H. ww1.habsburger.net/e

"First World War." Imperial War Museums iwm.org.uk/history/first-world-war

"National WWI Museum and Memorial." National WWI Museum and Memorial theworldwar.org

"World War One." The British Library, 23 Oct. 2013. bl.uk/world-war-one

RESOURCES

SELECTED BIBLIOGRAPHY

Eksteins, Modris. *Rites of Spring: The Great War and the Birth of the Modern Age*. Vintage Canada, 2012.

Englund, Will. *March 1917: On the Brink of War and Revolution*. W.W. Norton & Co., 2018.

Hochschild, Adam. *To End All Wars: A Story of Loyalty and Rebellion, 1914-1918*. Mariner, 2012.

Ives, Stephen, director. *American Experience: The Great War*. PBS, 2017.

MacMillan, Margaret. "The Rhyme of History: Lessons of the Great War." The Brookings Institution, 14 Dec. 2013. csweb.brookings.edu/content/research/essays/2013/rhyme-of-history.html

Martin, Rachel. *NPR American Chronicles: World War I*. Highbridge Audio, 2014.

Mombauer, Annika. "July Crisis 1914." International Encyclopedia of the First World War, 2018. encyclopedia.1914-1918-online.net/article/july_crisis_1914

Neuberger, Joan. "'It is a Wide Road that Leads to War.'" *Not Even Past*, University of Texas, Austin, Department of History, 12 Apr. 2014. notevenpast.org/it-is-a-wide-road-that-leads-to-war

Palmer, Svetlana, and Sarah Wallis. *Intimate Voices from the First World War*. HarperCollins, 2005.

Peck, Garrett. *The Great War in America: World War I and Its Aftermath*. Pegasus Books, 2020.

Winter, Jay. "How the Great War Shaped the World." *The Atlantic*, 9 Nov. 2018. theatlantic.com/magazine/archive/2014/08/how-the-great-war-shaped-the-world/373468

QR CODE GLOSSARY

Page 5: pbs.org/video/vault-world-war-i-posters-bcdgwr

Page 9: en.wikipedia.org/wiki/Lord_Kitchener_Wants_You#/media/File:30a_Sammlung_Eybl_Großbritannien._Alfred_Leete_(1882–1933)_Britons_(Kitchener)_wants_you_(Briten_Kitchener_braucht_Euch)._1914_(Nachdruck),_74_x_50_cm._(Slg.Nr._552).jpg

Page 9: en.wikipedia.org/wiki/Lord_Kitchener_Wants_You#/media/File:John_Bull_-_World_War_I_recruiting_poster.jpeg

Page 9: en.wikipedia.org/wiki/Lord_Kitchener_Wants_You#/media/File:Unclesamwantyou.jpg

Page 9: en.wikipedia.org/wiki/Lord_Kitchener_Wants_You#/media/File:Buy_Your_Victory_Bonds._Color_poster._Issued_by_Victory_Bond_Committee,_Ottawa,_Canada.,_ca._1917_-_NARA_-_516338.jpg

Page 9: en.wikipedia.org/wiki/Lord_Kitchener_Wants_You#/media/File:Bat_Zion_I_want_your_Old_New_Land_join_Jewish_regiment.jpg

Page 10: awm.gov.au/collection/ARTV00026

Page 10: awm.gov.au/collection/C101052

Page 10: npr.org/2019/01/06/682608011/after-falling-short-u-s-army-gets-creative-with-new-recruiting-strategy

Page 14: youtube.com/watch?v=HaG_JMxQ9eI&feature=youtu.be

RESOURCES

Page 16: avalon.law.yale.edu/19th_century/final99.asp

Page 19: commons.wikimedia.org/wiki/File:Scramble-for-Africa-1880-1913.png

Page 20: bl.uk/collection-items/europe-satirical-map

Page 25: rferl.org/a/princip-worldwar-terezin-sarajevo/25435831.html

Page 27: wwi.lib.byu.edu/index.php/The_Austro-Hungarian_Ultimatum_to_Serbia_(English_translation)

Page 28: serbia.com/about-serbia/serbia-history/world-war-one/slavka-mihajlovic

Page 33: ww1.habsburger.net/en/chaptersfirst-world-war-childs-play

Page 33: bl.uk/world-war-one/articles/childrens-experiences-and-propaganda

Page 37: eyewitnesstohistory.com/brussels.htm

Page 38: youtube.com/watch?v=WRTm7mw25WU&feature=youtu.be

Page 39: archives.gov/publications/prologue/1989/spring/hoover-belgium.html

Page 41: smithsonianmag.com/history/fleet-taxis-did-not-really-save-paris-germans-during-world-war-i-180952140

Page 43: iwm.org.uk/history/voices-of-the-first-world-war-the-christmas-truce

Page 46: youtu.be/DjqdgGb739w

Page 46: sueddeutsche.de/wissen/fotografie-im-ersten-weltkrieg-weltenbrand-in-farbe-1.1583330-3

Page 48: wdl.org/en/item/14724

Page 52: youtube.com/watch?v=EeEcyn6bA0E&feature=youtu.be

Page 53: nam.ac.uk/explore/wipers-times

Page 54: play.history.com/shows/wwi-the-first-modern-war/videos/the-germans-release-the-first-wmd

Page 56: storymaps.esri.com/stories/2015/uboats-in-ww1

Page 61: poetryfoundation.org/articles/70139/the-poetry-of-world-war-i

Page 62: npr.org/transcripts/7556326?storyId=7556326&storyId=7556326

Page 62: smithsonianmag.com/arts-culture/faces-of-war-145799854

Page 62: nam.ac.uk/explore/birth-plastic-surgery

Page 67: facinghistory.org/resource-library/video/introducing-armenian-genocide

Page 75: armenian-genocide.org/photo_wegner.html

Page 75: armenian-genocide.org/9-24-15.html

Page 75: npr.org/transcripts/7556326?storyId=7556326&storyId=7556326

Page 75: hrw.org

Page 79: digitalhistory.uh.edu/disp_textbook.cfm?smtID=3&psid=3898

Page 83: youtube.com/watch?v=qpslrJHp_6M&feature=youtu.be

Page 86: pbs.org/newshour/show/righting-wrong-nearly-100-years-later-two-soldiers-receive-medal-honor-posthumously

Page 87: youtube.com/watch?v=qpslrJHp_6M&feature=youtu.be

Page 90: youtube.com/watch?v=LlRtnEOeAnY&feature=youtu.be

Page 98: youtube.com/watch?v=UW5mXcjD4IQ

Page 106: npr.org/2011/11/11/142224795/the-bonus-army-how-a-protest-led-to-the-gi-bill

Page 107: shroudsofthesomme.com/news/85000-people-visit-shrouds-of-the-somme-in-london

Page 107: theguardian.com/artanddesign/2018/mar/05/how-we-made-tower-of-london-poppies-paul-cummins-tom-piper

Page 107: eturbonews.com/237730/massive-poppy-art-installation-a-must-see-in-munich-for-remembrance-day

INDEX

INDEX

S

satires, 13, 17, 20, 53
Schlieffen, Alfred von/Schlieffen
    Plan, 29, 30, 38
Serbia, vi, 3, 22–30, 31, 69
social unrest, 63–64. *See
    also* labor movements;
    women's movements
soldiers
    armistice reactions, 97, 100
    casualties. *See* casualties
    clothes, 46–47
    colonial or minority, 36,
        38, 60, 66, 86, 90
    mobilization of, 30, 31–32
    mutiny and desertion, 64,
        70, 73, 90, 96, 98
    photographs/images of, 4–6,
        28, 39, 43–45, 52–54,
        65, 83–84, 86, 100–101
    recruitment of, 2–3,
        7, 9–10, 31, 85
    training for combat, 82, 85, 89

T

tanks, vii, 50, 55–56
technologies. *See* military
    technologies and weapons
Treaty of Brest-Litovsk, vii, 74
Treaty of Versailles, vii, 99, 100
Trotsky, Leon, 73
Turkey, 31, 68, 69, 70–71

U

U-boats, vii, 50, 56, 57, 58, 82–83
United Kingdom. *See* Great Britain
United Nations, 103
United States, 77–93
    alliances, 78
    armistice and treaties,
        vii, 97, 99, 100
    economics of, 80, 103, 106
    entering the war, vii, 4,
        78–79, 83, 85
    home front, 86–88, 92
    immigrants and minorities
        in, 79, 80, 86, 87, 103
    music on war, 91–93
    neutrality stance, vii,
        4, 40, 78, 80–82
    propaganda campaigns,
        9, 86, 87
    public opinion on war,
        vii, 57, 77–78, 80–84,
        88, 91–93, 101
    soldiers, 31, 40, 79, 82–86,
        89–90, 100, 106
    tipping point for, 82–84
    Western Front role, 89–90
    World War I role, vii, 4,
        31, 40, 57, 77–93

W

weapons. *See* military
    technologies and weapons
Western Front, 35–48
    armistice and treaty, 96
    Belgium invasion, vi,
        30, 37–39, 48
    Christmas truce, vi, 43–45
    diversion from, 71
    France invasion, 30, 39–41
    military technologies and
        weapons, 50, 52–56

Miracle of Marne, vi, 40–41
preparations for war, 36
strategies, 30, 38, 39,
    40–41, 48, 54, 89–90
trench warfare, 35, 36,
    41–43, 50, 52–53
U.S. forces, 89–90
Wharton, Edith, 42
Wilhelm II, 15, 27, 31, 32, 97–98
Wilson, Woodrow, vii, 78–80,
    82–84, 92, 97, 99
women
    anti-war activism,
        80, 81, 84, 85
    pro-war activism, 32
    wartime roles, 8, 28,
        43, 66, 73, 88
    women's movements,
        13, 28, 32, 85, 103
World War I
    alliances. *See* alliances
    casualties. *See* casualties
    end of. *See* peace agreement
        and postwar developments
    fronts. *See* Eastern Front;
        Western Front
    name of, 6
    origins of, vi, 12–17, 21–34
    overview of, vi–vii, 3–4, 8
    soldiers in. *See* soldiers
    study of, 5–8
    United States and. *See*
        United States
    weapons. *See* military
        technologies and weapons
World War II, 96, 98,
    100, 101–102

Z

Zimmermann, Arthur/Zimmermann
    telegram, vii, 72, 84